2054

A COLLECTION OF SCI-FI NOVELLAS

YUDHANJAYA WIJERATNE   JT LAWRENCE
JASON WERBELOFF   COLBY R. RICE
FOREWORD BY SAMUEL PERALTA

FIRE FINCH

THE FUTURE IS NOW

Welcome to 2054, where memory hackers carve up your mind, sexbots lurk behind every corner, and the religious wear impenetrable skins.

Explore the ocean depths with AI-enhanced octopods.

Learn your past might not be what you remember.

Take a bot into your marriage bed.

Fall in love across an impenetrable divide.

FOREWORD

BY SAMUEL PERALTA

"Science has stolen most of our miracles."
— Scott Frank / Jon Cohen

The hotel in Santa Monica faced the ocean, its rectangular pool paint-chipped perfectly to the Pacific's blue.

The foyer was a mix of beach-chic California furniture, understated Spanish tile, and Italian chandeliers, punctuated by the occasional Acropora coral or David Hockney art piece.

Upstairs, you could open the windows and white wooden shutters in your room and invite the coastal breeze and sunset in; or step out onto the private balcony, Mimosa cocktail in hand, and take in the sweep of beach, the promenade and bicycle trail.

Half-an-hour drive away was Beverly Hills, the bustle of Hollywood—but here in the cradle of the Pacific, all that and the future seemed far away.

Here there was only the *now*.

The invitations came from Stewart Brand and Peter Schwartz.

Brand was a biologist and author, editor of the Whole Earth Catalog, and founder of the Long Now Foundation, which promotes a slower-and-better approach over today's faster-and-cheaper thinking. Their logo, a capital X with a bar over it, is the Roman numeral for 10,000. The foundation used 5-digit dates to address the Year 10,000 problem, and in that parlance, the year was not 1999, but 01999.

Schwartz was a futurist and author, and with Brand co-founded the Global Business Network, a firm specializing in corporate strategy and scenario planning.

A think tank, as it were, for the future.

Now Brand and Schwartz were convening a group of futurists and thinkers—leaders in their respective fields of architecture, physics, computer science, biology, politics, and socio-economics—to contribute to a special project.

The invitations went out to people like German conceptual automotive designer Harald Belker, architect and urban planner Peter Calthorpe, Canadian novelist and columnist Douglas Coupland, Cambridge fellow Joel Garreau, physicist and computer scientist Neil Gershenfeld of the Massachusetts Institute of Technology, biomedical researcher Shaun Jones, computer scientist and visual artist Jaron Lanier, Australian-born William J. Mitchell—known for the integration of architecture with computing and other technologies, and data interface and bioinformatics expert John Underkoffler.

People who could imagine the future.

Over three days in a Santa Monica hotel, they would

invent, in the parlance of the Long Now Foundation, the year 02054.

When Yudhanjaya Wijeratne approached me about "Project 2054"—a shared universe by himself and authors JT Lawrence, Jason Werbeloff and Colby R. Rice—my mind immediately leapt back to that other project almost twenty years ago, when a group of technologists and creative artists convened to put together their own template for the future.

Still over three decades away, MMLIV still seems as far away as it was back in 1999. And yet, much of the world foreseen by those futurists in their Pacific workshop has come true.

Computers controlled by point-and-touch gesture-recognition interfaces.

Self-driving, autonomous vehicles.

Hyper-personalized advertising that stores your preferences, tracking and targeting you across the Internet.

Voice-controlled home automation to control lights, play music, adjust the temperature.

Identity recognition through palm prints, retina scans, and A.I.-assisted facial recognition.

Predictive policing and law enforcement through big data and sociological analysis.

Ubiquitous surveillance systems.

Perhaps the most amazing, terrifying, breathtaking thing about all this is that much of the future predicted in 1999 has come true over forty years early.

Ironically, Steven Spielberg's 2002 neo-noir film *Minority Report* has itself become Exhibit A for one of its own central themes—precognition.

Its predictions for the future were built on round-table discussions from the Santa Monica summit, and distilled in the 2054 *Bible*, a detailed guide maintained by production designer Alex McDowell.

Working from a screenplay by Scott Frank and Jon Cohen, based on a 1956 short story by Philip K. Dick, Spielberg managed to orchestrate a film so immersive and real that, year after year, it has gotten more difficult to discern that invented future from our present.

What else is in that 2054 *Bible*, that 80-page guide that remains unpublished to this day? What precog visions does it contain, what prophecies failed to make it into Spielberg's onscreen storytelling?

There have been hints.

In an interview that Underkoffler had with *Salon* magazine, for example, he talked about autonomous media-bots, drones that collected audio-visuals of crime scenes, sporting events, or celebrity gatherings, competing with other drones for the best vantage points, and streaming the data back live to viewers.

Even this is coming true.

I imagine stories, many of them, emanating from the apocrypha of the 2054 *Bible*.

Stories set in a familiar world, yet different—constructed from the educated guesses, the precognition of authors who are also data scientists, philosophers, sociologists, and futurists—in the same spirit as the original conjuring of the world of 2054.

Stories about exploring the ocean depths with A.I.-enhanced cephalopods.

Stories about memory being tweezed and manipulated by genetic hackers.

Stories about intimate relationships between human and machine.

Stories about force-fields impermeable to everything except, perhaps, love.

Imagine a future that is at once amazing, terrifying, and breathtaking...

Imagine no more—the future is now.

Welcome to 2054.

— Samuel Peralta

Samuel Peralta is a physicist, entrepreneur, and storyteller. An award-winning author, he is the creator and driving force behind the bestselling speculative fiction anthology series The Future Chronicles.

www.samuelperalta.com

DEEP OCEAN BLUES

YUDHANJAYA WIJERATNE

IN THE BAY OF BENGAL, NO ONE CAN
HEAR YOU SCREAM.

When Parul signed up to work on Rig #443 thousands of
feet beneath the ocean, she expected to make it out
unharmed.

But bitter truths lurk in the depths ... and soon Parul's
survival is at stake.

DEEP OCEAN BLUES

PICTURE THE OCEAN on a stormy night.

Wave fronts breaking under the storm. Water tossing, turning, frothing, a heaving mass of black that was once blue. A deepness so vast and so profound it would crush your bones long before you even hit the bottom.

Go down.

Past the point where men drown and the thunder and lightning fade to dim flashes on the other side of murky ink.

Past the point where fish swim in the darkness and strange things float by among the ghosts of the submarines that once fought in the Bay of Bengal.

On the ocean floor, there is light again. A sort of neon pink haze that sparks and flickers on the grey ocean floor. A Bubble. One of the cheap kind, the stuff they give to miners. Bootlegged Israeli tech, or maybe Chinese; who knows. Bought cheap and rebadged by the Bay Of Bengal Corporation. It shimmers and wraps itself around the mining rig at the bottom of the ocean, a little disco for eyeless fish. The thump-thump-thump of thorium minescoops reverb through the heavy ocean water.

Inside is Parul Anand, Operator, Rig #443. She stumbles against the waterlock, her short, dark hair matted with something that could be oil, could be blood. In her right hand is a photo of the fiancé she left behind. Or maybe he left her; it is hard to remember. It's hard to remember because one of her other arms is clutching a bottle of moonshine. Home-brewed rig junk. Two thirds of it is already in her system.

Even her body, re-engineered for the pressures of the job, cannot cope with this stuff. Parts of her are slurring. Other parts blink red.

It's Valentines day.

And, like every other day down here, it's a very lonely one.

IF WE HAD A PENCIL, and a good map, and a certain willingness to make giant leaps of fact, we could trace the path that lead Parul here. We could say it began in 2020, when the world had too many people and the oil was running out faster than expected; we could trace a line from that to the research poured out by the scientists of the time, who spoke of thorium, the safe, atomic fuel that lay off the coasts of India and Sri Lanka, the fuel that could not be weaponized the way uranium could.

The line would skitter and skid across the wars that ravaged the Bay of Bengal - India and China throwing submarines and missiles at each other, fighting cold, fast and furious proxy wars to determine who would control the future of energy on the Earth. And then we would get to the 2040s, when brave explorers of the deep, blessed by temporary truces, cast off into the depths. They sent messages back to the surface about the abundant reserves of thorium and hydrosulphates that lay just below the ocean bed - and died horrible deaths when Rig #1 sprung a leak and collapsed in on itself.

We could trace lines all day - from discovery to commercialization, from national to corporate interests, from brave new world to yet another high-risk blue collar job.

Or we could trace the line of Parul: born to Sri Lankan and Indian parents, a citizen of both countries and welcome in neither. Grew up on the coast of Jaffna. Studied hard, kept her head down, made it to university. One of India's top ten colleges, too. Found a good Indian boy to settle down with.

And blew it all when it turned out the good Indian boy had been cheating on her throughout their relationship. Took a job that took away from her all of the pain and suffering and torment of Topside and gave her months of intense psych conditioning and sent her down four kilometers to the bottom of the ocean, the only human being in the beating heart of a great automated operation leeching the ocean bed dry of that precious fuel.

All paths would eventually lead to hundreds of rigs dotting the ocean floor, busy churning out fuel for the human race, and Parul Anand trapped here in #443, held in place by a contract and thousands of tons of water pressing down on her.

It was a token job. #443, like all the other rigs owned by the Corporation, ran itself. Thorium is three times as abundant as uranium; much of it, readily mineable, exists in the form of monazite, two-thirds of which are off the south and east coasts of India. An army of SubMiners skitters around the main drill sites, teasing out and sorting ore. Every day they bring back precious monazite to the beating heart of the rig - a vast refinement complex that sunk deep concrete roots into the ocean floor and runs with a steady *thump-thump-thump*, cooled by the water itself. A squad of jury-rigged OctoPods - poor critters - keeps an eye on the outermost perimeter, where communication lines could be compromised by debris. Every so often an automated transport shuttle, guarded by submarines, does the rounds, picks up fuel, and departs.

Parul, like all other human operators, is only there because BIMSTEC regulations require a human presence on board any automated system above a particular size. The only other living things attached to #443 are the OctoPods. They float like ghostly, tentacled guardians, occasionally beeping in distress when the electronic mind of #443 takes control and steers them and their sensor arrays to areas where it suspects damage.

Beep. Beep.

Line status OK.

And, listening to this exchange, sits Parul, feeling the crushing loneliness envelop her, heavier sometimes than the ocean itself. When this is done, she's going to have her brain wiped. Get one of those bio-hackers to keep just a few glimpses of this whole experience and replace everything else with glittering, beautiful fakes. There could be entire cities down here, New Yorks and Delhis glittering in the ocean -

SHE WAKES up to the alarm and crawls upright, the hangover pounding a tattoo in her skull. She's in the Front Bay, what she thinks of as the Living Room. It's painfully bright - whoever designed the rigs had set the bloody day-night cycle in stone. The light reflects painfully off the dome and returns with an electric pink glow from the Bubble outside.

"Rise and shine!" says the Rig from speakers embedded in the walls. It's meant to be cheery, but three hundred days of hearing the same thing in the exact same voice with the exact same intonation have taken their toll. To Parul it is little more than some dreadful white noise.

She pulls herself to her feet slowly, servomotors whining. Her mouth stinks. The air smells of sweat and cheap booze. The mechanical arms grafted onto her back keep her upright as she sets off, swaying, in a slow and methodical cycle around the domed room, sweeping aside the spills, checking the waterlock seals, righting the one chair she has in the Front Bay.

The Bay has a roughly rectangular layout with a pool in the center, almost as deep as she is tall. The pink light turns it black. It's supposed to be for the OctoPods, but she slides into it with a muffled groan, letting the water take some of the weight away from her body.

She is tired. It's a low kind of tiredness, the kind that creeps up in the head, that takes the color away from the world and replaces it with dreariness.

"Breakfast," she says. Her voice barely rises above a scratchy whisper.

"Right away," says #443. The kitchen rumbles to life. "Ready, Miss Anand. Shall we review the logs?"

"In a bit," she says, enjoying the lull of the water. It is nice and warm. Outside the world is grey.

Eventually she pulls herself out and pads over to the kitchen, dripping. The kitchen is small and made mostly of metal. In the oven is bread from yesterday, heated to bearable levels. On a tray under the dispenser is the greenish goop #443 serves for breakfast. Something powdered. It's supposed to taste like meat, but to Parul it has always tasted like salted papier-maché, or unsalted scrambled eggs cooked without butter. The smell of tea - not proper tea, but some harmless weed-herb drowned in water - comes from the electric pot nearby.

Perks of setting things up before you get wasted. She sets the tray down on the cold metal table, sits on a stool that creaks gently under her weight, and eats.

"Shall we review the logs?" says #443, insistent.

She makes the gesture that the rig has now learned to interpret as *later,* or, in serious cases, *shut up.* The bread is warm and crunches gently in her mouth. It wraps the goop in an almost buttery taste. The tea clears her throat. Bread. Goop. Tea. The cycle slowly brings her to life, reduces the headache. She flexes her extra arms as she eats, running them through the same exercises athletes do to warm up. The arms are technically company property - they, like the rig, are stamped with BoB insignia - but to Parul, as to all Operators, they're part of her body now. Say what you will about the BoB, but they do good bodywork.

She wonders idly if they will let her keep this body once the contract is done. Imagine coming home with these beauties. Her parents would be horrified. Look, Ma, new muscle.

She catches a glimpse of her reflection in the metal table-top. Short, chopped hair, grunge marks on her cheeks. A sort of hollow, haunted look. They would be horrified even without the arms.

Ironic. She's named for a flower. If there ever was anything flower-like in her, there's nothing left. Certainly not in this shell.

"Let's see those reports now," she says. Her vision is immediately crowded with figures, charts, details. The rig plays white noise in the background while she reads. A line of red failure warnings draw her attention.

"What's up with 3B?"

Her view zooms in; ghostly lines trace themselves over the walls, the floor, the furniture. They show her a long power line snaking across the ocean floor and, floating alongside it, Octopod 3B: a soft grey ghostlike thing with many arms. It appears to be listing to one side.

Parul studies it, trying to figure out which part is octopus, which part is mechanical, and which is failing. Another Octopod has been dispatched to replace 3B, but it will take some time to arrive.

"Bring him in."

Communication lines pulse. 'Pod 3B chirrups a series of beeps - sounds like pain - and makes a slow, erratic turn. It begins walking back across the ocean floor to #443, beeping softly all the while. A counter springs up in her vision: ETA 30 MINUTES.

Thirty minutes is a long time in Rig-hours (or a short time, depending on what you're feeling like; Rig time is funny that way). She decides to check on the greenhouse while they wait for the Octopod. She eats as she walks; the ramp from the kitchen to Technical, two lefts, two flights of stairs up - her company-built arms grip the railings and propel her up with almost savage ease - and there we are: the greenhouse. A hot, sweltering dome filled with UV lamps. It turns her skin from golden-brown to the darkest, deepest black. The trees guard row upon row of vegetables and modified oxygen-plants.

She likes coming up here: there's very little she can actually do, but it's nice to be among other things that live.

The trees have a noise of their own; the noise of life grow-ing. On particularly bad days she imagines she can hear a soft rustling, like a breeze shaking the tender stalks - an improbable wind many fathoms in the deep.

But even here the tiredness strikes, she knows; stay long enough in one place, and eventually it too becomes dull and dreary. And so she creeps back, carefully rationing her trips to that green field under the violet lights.

OCTOPOD 3B TAKES a long time to arrive. Too long. He should have been there by the time she reached the waterlock, but instead he's two hundred meters away from the entrance, struggling mightily.

Alarmed, she switches to the biomonitor. Rigs have a tendency to burn through OctoPods - word is the average 'Pod lasted five months before the electrodes and receivers implanted in its brain drove it mad. Some 'Pods killed them-selves; others had to be given the Kill signal, a short, sharp burst that would fry the tender neurons and turn the little creature into a husk. The next 'Pod would retrieve the corpse.

Parul doesn't approve of it, but the 'Pods are effective and cheap; they breed like little undersea rabbits. And when fitted with a decent harness and mechanical arms they can keep the pipes running like clockwork. Eight legs, three hearts, that crazy distributed intelligence, excellent naviga-tion skills - better a creature adapted to life at 4,000 feet than a human being flailing its arms in the darkness, as the company said. Those who disagreed faced the prospect of piloting drone subs or hiking out themselves with nothing but a thing layer of glass between them and the ocean. No sir.

So Parul accepts the system and does the next best thing: she keeps them fed, happy, and alive. Her OctoPods tended to last twice as long as the average. And they give her something to talk to every so often, even if that something doesn't understand.

This one - 3B - is old, practically a pensioner by human standards. He's had trouble before with the harness. He beeps softly as he approaches the waterlock, weaving slightly. She crosses the pool to peer through the glass at him. He seems to be having trouble opening the door; his tentacles reach for locks that aren't there, and when he finds the right one it takes him two organic arms and one mechanical to open it. The beeping is insistent; it's their sign of distress.

He sloshes into the waterlock.

She dims the lights. 'Pods are used to the crushing darkness of the water outside: human-friendly illumination would drive them blind.

"Draining lock for OctoPod levels," announces #443. The waterlock drain until the OctoPod is in three feet of water, maybe four, and then the whole thing, Pod and all, is emptied into the pool.

Close up, an OctoPod is a startling thing: a small grey-purple octopus wrapped in company black. It thrashes in the water, its movements magnified and sketched out in the air by the pincer and welder arms that erupt from the harness. Black, beady eyes regard her with unfathomable emotion. A soft mass of suckers writhe at her. The slender, eight-limbed body is run through with wires and electrodes, merging the creature and the harness, allowing the rig to replace its natural cravings - food, mating - with the need to repair and report.

He beeps at her. Out of the water, it's a surprisingly loud pulse, like an explosion of sonar against her eardrums.

"Hey, hey, calm down, calm *down*," she croons, reaching out, offering her hands. "I'm here. You're safe. 443? Give me a sedative."

Two tentacles wrap themselves around her hands and give them a gentle squeeze. There is a moment of contact, this strange, rubbery creature reaching out to her for comfort, and then the sedative in the water kicks in. There is one last pulse. 3B falls asleep.

"Take him to the surgery," she says, feeling like a butcher standing over her prize. "Let's see what's wrong with him."

THE COLD, glaring lights of the surgery tell her what she'd suspected. It is the electrodes. Buried deep into the octopus's neural structure, they have started burning out tissue around them - there are pockets of dead neurons everywhere she looks. If the octopus is lucky, the electrodes burn out some part of the comms infrastructure, and it gets to keep its fancy company arms and harness; Parul is pretty sure there's at least a dozen critters with their mechanical arms out there running free in the deep.

But that's the best case scenario. Most times the neural damage turns the creature into a brain-dead vegetable.

"Surgery," she orders. "Keep the octopus alive, detach the harness."

There is a pause, as if the rig is surprised by the request.

"Surgery is deemed non-essential for OctoPods," it advises cautiously. "This system recommends letting OctoPod 3B die and simply transferring the electrodes from the dead body into a new octopus."

"I said, surgery."

Once again that pause. "OctoPod surgery is not authorized by Topside, except in the case of post-mortem analysis. Should you wish to order this service, the costs will have to be debited from the Operator's funds."

"Just do the damn surgery!" she shrieks at it. A raised voice from her is rare, and even the AI holds its contempt at bay and spins up the autodoctor. Glass and metal parts slide out from the sides and interlock to form a sealed chamber. Inside, slender mechanical arms unfold hover over the octopod. Lasers begin cutting into the tender flesh. Soon they will start pulling out the first of three hundred slim wafers from the scar tissue. It reminds her of a giant metal spider, crouched - and the image is both disturbing and funny, because of the number of limbs involved.

"May I ask why you are doing this?" says #443 from a speaker near her, quieter now.

"Can't just let him die, 443," she says. It's difficult to explain. Even here, at the bottom of the world, even for something as fundamentally alien as an octopus, there is some pity for a creature that suffers.

"Even in the event of survival, it is unlikely that the specimen will adapt to life on its own," says 443. "The urge to explore, to report, will have by now become part of its adult programming. This is an exercise with very poor return on investment."

"How much is this going to cost me?" she asks.

A number flashes in her vision. She winces. That's two months' salary. Is an OctoPod worth a month of her time? No wonder #443 thought she was mad.

This is Parul, doing good and regretting it almost immediately after.

THE SURGERY TAKES NEARLY seven hours, during which she has time to think. The water in the pool is still laced with powerful sedative, so she fills the back waterlock and floats in it, letting the water hold her suspended. She is dangerously close to the Outside - just one glass door away is the ocean floor, lit grey by #443's flood-lamps. In here, in water, there is no rush, no tension, just thought. In the distance is the golden flicker of Rig #432 - an older operation, much better equipped.

Dear Ma, she thinks. *Today I saved an OctoPod.*

She imagines the thought escaping her, floating gently out from the rig, and rising to the surface in a bubble.

It cost me a lot.

And what would her mother say? Parul had no idea. Probably something nasty about her life choices. Parul's mother, like most mothers, has a very strict view of the way the world should work. Parul had been the smart one - she was supposed to be the kid who would have a superstar career, marry well, and bring a luxurious end-of-life to her elderly parents. None of that has happened. Parul's parents are instead left to manipulate their other children into being their retirement plans, and Parul has long since gone from being expected and welcome to being unexpected and ridiculed.

The water is warm and comfortable. That's #443, heating it, unasked. In many ways the rig is a better parent than most actual parents she knows.

She meditates upon how strange the world is. Far above her, on the waters of the Bay of Bengal, battleships prowl, guarding invisible lines in an uneasy truce; messages fly at the speed of light between India and Sri Lanka, and among the uncountable millions of bits is a question: *Have you seen my daughter?*

The OctoPod takes days to recover. She can't imagine what it's like to spend your entire life as a slave to the Rig - Sri Lankan parents are close, but at least they don't turn you into a lobotomized lump of jelly.

It's a choice of watch the octopus or watch yet another canned TV series, so she watches it daily. Parts of the harness are still attached - the mechanical arms, the speakers.

Not for the first time, she wonders how the company managed to get the scientific testing acts overthrown. Like all Rig operators, she had gone through extensive slides on the octopus. They were a protected species until the thorium mines happened. Two-thirds of the brain in the arms, and suction cups that can taste at the same time they touch; she wonders what that would be like - to have touch and taste woven so tightly together than they are just one sense; it must be like having tongues for hands. And with those hands they could build little fortresses underwater, and carry tools for many miles to repair undersea pipes.

A Nobel prize winner once said that octopuses were the first intelligent creatures. Parul thinks it is also one of the loneliest creatures on earth - just a big brain with eight arms and three hearts, dumped in the ocean, no schools, no groups, no parents around to teach it anything; a big baby left to learn about the world from scratch.

Slowly the tentacles stir, and slowly the neurons in the arms and in the center mass start rearranging themselves. 3B looks around, still sluggish under the sedatives. she wonders if it feels like she did when she woke from the company surgery with two extra arms.

"Hey, 3B," she tries, trailing an arm into the tank.

The horizontal slits fix on her, and the hand. Slowly a tentacle reaches out, trying to grasp her hand. It misses. She catches it, and 3B gives her hand a gentle squeeze. It beeps softly, once.

ON THE SECOND DAY, he tried to escape.

Parul had been warned about this by #443. She hurries down from her daily greenhouse escape to find 3B thrashing about. He's gotten the use of his mechanical arms back now; somehow, he's fiddled with the pool cover and wrapped himself around the table. His skin is a blotchy reddish-black. When he sees her, he squirts. Black liquid rains around the table.

"I told you this would happen," says #443. The rig sounds both smug and resigned. A couple of housekeeping bots unfold from the walls and, with Parul running the perimeter, they manage to herd 3B back into the pool, where he retreats to the furthest corner, quivering. Parul, feeling sorry for him, rummages in the kitchen for some plastic bowls and drops them into the pool. Arms shoot out and arrange them around 3B like plates. Slit eyes peer out from between them.

"Told you," says #443.

They let him go on the third day. Actually, #443 lets him go: the rig slips it into the morning log review. *Specimen 3B returned to the outside for further evaluation of post-surgery cephalapod regeneration.* Looking over the log trails, Parul realizes that #443, unasked, has written off the surgery as an experiment for company research purposes.

"Thanks for saving my cash," she says, feeling grateful towards this big, thinking dome that she lives in.

The tracker shows 3B heading slowly determinedly away from the rig.

"You're welcome," says #443 gently. "May we proceed to the Update?"

The company does this in batches: whatever news she subscribes to, whatever social feeds - they'll cache it and send it over once every two weeks. It's more than possible to be connected all the time, because many of lines that run to the rig carry data - but ten years of studies have shown that Operators, in isolation, become terrible social media gluttons, almost to the point of wasting away; some of them become neurotic. This is safer. This way, even if she goes mad in here, she can't damage the company brand.

This Update is huge. Social feeds - she checks those first - more of the usual. Some of her friends are getting married. The few whose parents are rich enough that they don't need to pay rent for a few years - they're traveling. Photos from Hong Kong, Egypt, South Africa, Neo-Tokyo. All places she wants to see someday, but probably never will on this salary.

Bank statements. Pay-checks. Rent deposits to her parents' accounts: at least they can't say she never paid her keep. Purchases and wishlists. That remouldable sexbot she's been keeping her eye on has appeared on the market again. It's supposed to be better than having an actual guy or girl in bed. A few taps and it's bought, paid for and delivered to her Delhi address. There's some amount of money left, growing steadily, enough for a place of her own once she gets topside.

And then the news. Parul scans the feeds, frowning. Something serious is happening Topside. Chinese aircraft carriers sending out drones on training exercises near the Nepal border. Upswings of nationalism in India; talk of China's expansionism; talk of taking control over the new

Silk Road. Accusations that Sri Lanka is harboring Chinese military submarines. Myanmar and Thailand vowing to send forth fleets 'to preserve the peace' if the delicate China-BIMSTEC trade agreements are disrupted.

Hostilities are never good, but this is particularly bad. Two of the largest stakeholders in the Bay of Bengal Corporation are Indian and Chinese companies. Of course they're supposed to be private - but everyone knows CHEC is controlled by the Chinese government and Indian Oil & Energy is owned by the state.

She reads further. America, always eager to meddle in IndoChina, has presented a carefully prepared statement at the UN, that, if read between the lines, say *we'll sit this one out and watch the fireworks from a safe distance, thank you.*

"Maadher chod," she swears.

"If it is of any consolation, our asset value is too high to be ignored," says #443, who has no doubt read the feeds and then some. "We'll either be sold or extracted long before something happens."

"You mean *your* asset value is too high," Parul reminds the rig. "I'm just a human. There's billions of us."

To this even #443 has no answer.

Parul spends an inordinate amount of time at the greenhouse that day, thinking. The UV light turns her into a dark shadow moving between the plants.

The only way to deal with this, she decides, is to go on. There's not much she can do; she's filed a video message to a few close friends asking them if she should quit - she'll forfeit the completion bonus on her contract, and it's a hefty sum, so it's not a decision to take lightly. Her family is probably safe.

She breaks protocol to reach out to #432 - it's a large rig: there should be at least two people there.

"Hey," she says over the voice-only channel. "I know this is illegal, but are you there?"

A clipped Australian voice answers. "Ah, fuck legal. We were wondering when you'd hit us up. Maggie, Vinu, c'mere."

They talk. It only takes a few minutes for them to warm to each other. Parul lets go of the tension in her chest, the fear of a gruff voice descending and cutting the line. They're impressed by how long she's been there without talking to them. She's impressed by how comfortable they seem with each other, how they finish each other's sentences, how they navigate the job without throwing each other out of waterlocks.

"It's probably just bluster," says Vinu, who seems to be the oldest of them. "Neither of them want a war, it's just hand-waving. There's probably some major deal going in and someone wants a bit more political clout."

"We're sitting on enough thorium to power cities for a few hundred years. Easiest way to cripple India is take us out."

"But we also supply to China. They've got major thorium running their grid."

"Has anyone spoken about us?"

The sound of headsets being put on and feeds being checked.

"Nah," said the Australian voice from the deep. "Let's just keep our heads down, hope they forget us. Check back next week?"

It seems prudent.

She heads for the kitchen, rifling through the drawers for her ganja stash. Two of her arms roll while the others absent-minded scratch her head. She doesn't normally smoke, because there's only so much stress you should put on the air recycler, but the greenhouse explicitly had a few marijuana plants with a marker saying "for special cases." This is a special case.

She heads for the greenhouse, almost by reflex, but corrects herself and walks the other way, out from the kitchen, to the other side of what she thinks of as the living room. There is a door here that she's only supposed to open twice in her entire stay here: once to check, and once to escape. It looks like serious business - triple layers of security: biometrics and voice-recog locks and an additional hidden authorization from #443 itself.

The door hisses. The thump of bolts been driven back echo from inside it. It slides neatly to the right.

Inside are what look like three medpods. Unlike the rest of the rig, this room is a stark, clinical white. Blue lines run alongside the pods. Two of them have a complex needleset of electrodes bristling inside. These are for sending pulses of electrical activity into a brain, reading the patterns, and storing them. The other pod has heavy-duty pipes running into it, and is a 3D printer.

She walks gingerly to this third pod, remembering what it was like to be born in it. Topside, two years ago; an office as clean and clinical as this room, filled as far as the eye can see with machines just like this. THE SOUL IS IN THE SOFTWARE, says a sad attempt at a slogan, just belong the BoB logo.

"It'll be fine," says the doctor with the bored, mask-like face. It feels like he's said this many, many times before. "We'll keep your Original on ice, once your contract's up, you cast back in, good as new. When you get there your rig will brief you on the emergency cast protocols."

The needles bristle and move to make room for her. She

remembers the brief terror as gas floods the chamber, putting her to sleep.

Somewhere along the line there had been magic. The electrode machine had read her brain patterns, packaged them, beamed them down to #443, which patiently awaited its new Operator. The body printer went into action, building an almost-identical body replica of Parul Anand, 23. Well, maybe not ideal. A bit better adapted for life underwater, with a couple of extra hands . . .

And the next thing she knows, she is inside this pod, miles below the surface of the ocean, with two extra arms and a ringing headache. Here. Gasping for breath in a body that had only existed for a week. Her real body on ice. When her time her is done, she will step into one of these pods and wake up Topside, puking her guts out, feeling ghost limbs where two extra arms used to be. A death here, a life there. It is the cheapest option in a world where cheap options are the only options.

This is her only way in, and her only way out.

Two of her hands clutch the ganja cigar. The other two tap the metal surface of the printer, *tap tap tap tap tap*.

The Australian is right. Keeping their heads down is the only thing any of them can do. There is no possibility of escape.

TO DISTRACT HERSELF, she starts reading up on octopus intelligence. Among the vast library that #443 has to stave off boredom is a near-complete dump of Wikipedia.

Cephalopod intelligence. *The cephalopod class of molluscs, particularly the Coleoidea subclass (cuttlefish, squid, and octopuses), are thought to be the most intelligent invertebrates and an important example of advanced cognitive evolution in animals.*

The scope of cephalopod intelligence is controversial, complicated by the elusive nature and esoteric thought processes of these creatures. In spite of this, the existence of impressive spatial learning capacity, navigational abilities, and predatory techniques in cephalopods is widely acknowledged.

One of the slidesets they went through in Basic Training was called "the Octopus: the First Predator". In it, a low-budget anim showed a prehistoric sea creature – something like a cross between a hermit crab and a snail. Slowly, the waving fronds became tentacles; the shell disappeared. While on land things continued to evolve and kill each other, the anim octopus quickly hit a basic form, and diversified. Little octopuses, big octopuses, octopuses with long arms, octopuses that kept the frond-like tentacles.

"Remember," the slide had ended by saying. "this is the first predator."

Company fear-mongering. Scare the new recruits a bit: makes it easier to get them to obey. It takes a month or so down here to realize that the scary-looking rubbery things are weird, but basically nicer than most people.

The Wikipedia article agrees. It says very little about predatory behavior. Instead, she reads about Maximilian, the German octopus who would pick up rocks and beat them against the walls of his tank in an erratic tap-tap-tap whenever certain visitors were nearby. They initially thought it was aggression, but a curious Japanese researcher thought it was more.

It turns out Maximilian the octopus had built up some sort of language influenced by the pulsing of the projector lamps right in front of him, like some sort of pseudo-Morse code. Unfortunately they never figured out what all of it meant, because Maximilian died shortly after they deciphered the tap-taps for 'food' and 'anger'.

She reads about Colony8, one of the only three octopus colonies ever found, where generations of octopuses had built, rebuilt and expanded their dens out of whatever was lying around, until the final result was a sort of octopus Troy. When the first human divers found Colony8, one particularly large octopus actually gave them a tour of the place, like an eight-armed parent shepherding a bunch of children through her study. Every so often, the divers noted, a lonely octopus reaches out of its den with one tentacle, and if there was a friend nearby it would reach back.

She stumbles across the page for Synthetic, the first octopus to have 'trodes stuck on them. Pulses of electrical activity were turned into patterns for researchers to see. They reverse the flow: can we tell it what to think, and will it understand? And thus the first octopus to be able to truly communicate with humans lobotomizes itself by bashing its head repeatedly against the glass wall of its tank. Its limbs take hours to die.

She reads about how Humboldt squid coordinate their hunting by flashing colors very rapidly at each other, too fast for the human eye to see, swimming at over 20 kilometers with arms lined with razor-sharp teeth.

Her searching becomes pseudorandom in itself, stumbling every so often across things she already knows. The octopus's slit-eye has no blind spot, for example. In the human eye, the optic nerve is a thick tree interrupting the layer of detector cells in the eye. Nerve fibers run over the surface of the retina, so light passes through a layer of nerves before hitting the detector cells; that seems a very stupid way of doing things. In contrast, the octopus eye is the right way around: detector cells, then nerve cells, no interruptions. In fact, everything about the octopus seems right compared to the lowly human. Eight arms; three hearts; a body that's ugly, but capable of almost anything.

"If we can make contact with cephalopods as sentient beings, it is not because of a shared history, not because of kinship, but because evolution built minds twice over," says Godfrey-Smith, the bio-philosopher, on repeat. "This is probably the closest we will come to meeting an intelligent alien."

Parul wonders, not for the first time, how humans ended up owning the cephalopods, and not the other way around. Pardon me, madam, have you heard of our lord and savior, Cthulhu?

"You should see this," says #443. jarring her out of her reverie.

Perhaps the rig is tired of watching its human do nothing. "What's happening?"

Her eyefeed activates. It's 3B. He's somewhere on the ocean floor, some distance away from the rig – and he seems to be hovering near an undersea cable of some sort. In his hand-tentacles he clutches an autowrench. He taps the cable gently with the 'wrench. Parul recognizes what he's doing: it's an OctoPod checking a line for defects.

The camera zooms out, pans. A foot away from the OctoPod is a downed repair drone. Painted Tata colors. Its head looks punched in, as if two mechanical arms -

"Oh, hell," says Parul. "Did 3B do that?"

"Looks like it," says #443. "A bill for damages arrived five minutes ago. According to Tata's footage, one of our 'Pods was caught repairing their line. The drone identified it as a threat and tried to evict it, and it, quote, "went batshit crazy and beat seven kinds of hell out of the drone. We appreciate repairs, but not vigilante repairmen."

She snorts. "That's actually hilarious."

"This is," says #443, "not a laughing matter."

It is, though. "What are we doing about 3B?"

"I considered using a SubMiner to finish him off, but decisions regarding the taking of life are the Operator's," says #443. The footage changes, shows an OctoPod scuttling after a yellow SubMiner. "As is, I flashed lights a couple of times and got 3B to follow. It seems to be quite eager to get back to work."

Parul thinks about it. It seems callous to kill the Octo-Pod. 3B had worked the line for months until the 'trode damage got to him. Besides, it looked like he wanted something to work on.

"Bring him in again," she orders the rig.

WITHOUT THE 'TRODES, shepherding 3B should have been difficult, but it isn't: he readily follows the SubMiner to the waterlock, creeps in, and waits the usual lock-to-pool process. His skin is dark and shot through with a pattern of ovals and veins.

She has #443 run a preliminary scan while they wait, and stares at the OctoPod. He, splayed out in the rapidly-emptying waterlock, stared back, and touches the glass between them with a tentacle. She raises a hand on her side. His skin changes, going to what she thinks of as their happy colors: a pale, almost uniform whitish-purple. The mechanical arms open and shut.

"He seems docile," says #443. "It will, however, take much observation to determine if there is neurological damage."

Inside the pool-tank, the octopus stares at her with his slit-eyes, skin changing anxiously from red to grey and back again.

"How do we deal with this?"

"If we are to execute him, you must give me the command," says #443. "I can sedate him via the tank and stop his hearts. It will be painless. Shall we?"

"I . . ." Parul's mouth goes dry.

"It would be best to dispose of it now, without further waste of company resources," suggests #443.

Parul swallows. "Can we keep him for a few more days?"

"And do what?"

"Maybe we can release him if he's stable. Take the arms. Let him go free."

"This is a waste of company resources and may have to be deducted from your payment," says the rig. "This facility is meant to operate OctoPods, not care for them."

Parul thinks of the way the OctoPod touched the glass, just now, and was happy. It keeps staring at her. "I don't think we should kill him just because we can," she says. "I think we should figure out what's wrong with him and see if we can help. I don't know. At least give it a shot."

#443 makes an odd noise. "Very well," it says. Parul gets the impression that the rig is exasperated with her.

THROUGHOUT THE NEXT FEW DAYS, as Parul wakes up anxiously and re-reads the feeds, the rig works.

First there is the daily schedule, of course: these things must be maintained regardless of what happens Topside. A little under six hundred tons of monazite pass each day into the rig. The process is slowed down, of course, by so many things - the water itself, making it difficult for SubMiners to move fast, increasing their energy expenditure; the constant need for repairs; the endless safety and ore purification checks. But #443 adjusts things so that the quota is met every day. Three Hannibal units constantly lead a squad of SubMiners to map out new veins and deposits; these are calculated, optimal navigation parts established, and the rig continues its cycle of production.

Once this is done, #443 considers the OctoPod. First the mechanical arms must be stripped away: those are too dangerous to have lying around. It is a slow operation, made slower by the need of tender flesh to recover.

#443 was not being truly precise with the Operator when it said this facility was not built for the care and feeding of OctoPods. Every rig is armed with a variant of SubMiners that can capture and conduct the underwater surgery needed to replace the OctoPods that die. #443 weighs the costs of rerouting one and installing it indoors versus the benefits of keeping its human Operator busy and engaged with this OctoPod case. The Operator has been stressed as of late: she has been smoking more marijuana and spending more time in the garden. The rig is not a psychotherapist, but in its vast data structure is a comprehensive analysis of what humans do when stressed (smoke too much), how they operate under stress (not very well), and how Operator stress significantly impairs a rig's efficiency.

Costs: minor. Benefits: major.

And so a Hannibal Unit (a strange name for a robotic hunter-doctor, but human nomenclature appears to follow very few set schemes) is diverted, brought in via the secondary waterlock, disassembled and reassembled in the room housing the body printer. The arms are slowly disassembled and cut out, and the octopus placed under sedative and steroids to help the healing. By the time the octopus wakes, the full set – the electrodes, the arms – are re-registered on the rig inventory as *available, pending new octopus*.

Meanwhile, the process that engages with the Operator is cloned, given access to the OctoPod lexicon, and tasked with dealing with Specimen 3B. Human Operators often guess at, but rarely come to know the full dictionary of the OctoPod language of beeps and color-changes. The specimen responds well within parameters. It is curious, hungry, responds to the right set of beeps and room color changes with pleasure.

The loss of its mechanical arms do not deter it. Octopuses do not possess a somatotopic map of their limbs the way humans do: the octopus nervous system, designed to deal with a number of limbs with practically unlimited flexibility, delegates motor control to the arms themselves. An octopus is only vaguely aware of its arms – it just had a series of little independent tentacles that rush to do the bidding of the central brain, like semi-intelligent minions. Waking up with fewer arms puzzle the specimen, but do not cause major trauma.

Beep beep beeeeep, it says, puzzled, swirling around.

Beep, responds #443, a single blaring note. The voxcoder in the OctoPod's harness translates. Specimen 3B settles down.

Thus engrossed, neither the rig nor the former OctoPod nor the human operator notices the bombs that fall.

The first wave is unleashed by an Indian submarine. The INS Aridhaman is an Arihant-II class submarine. The original Arihant was one of India's first nuclear submarines – a fast attacker that raised new fears about India's rising military capabilities. This one is new, almost freshly minted, and so is the crew. They are men on high alert, stressed to the boiling point with nerves and the news that China has declared hostilities towards India – not all-out war, but border skirmishes to prove a point.

They have been told to watch out for Chinese deep-dive submarines scouting the thorium mining network that keeps India running. And they have detected one, or they think they have: a Chinese sub running almost noiselessly through the dark. They have been tailing it for a while now, mostly by gut feel and good luck. Neither submarine dares ping each other for fear of confirming their presence.

The Chinese submarine in question is a People's Liberation Army Navy Type 102-V. It has been sent not to damage the thorium network, but to drop a network of its own – autonomous undersea missile launchers that can conduct what the Chinese call a *phantom strike* in the event of war. Its crew is much more experienced, and its captain is aware of the Indians trailing them through the darkness.

Finally, once twenty-four of their launchers have been dropped, the Chinese submarine coasts to a place far away from their mission and pings the Indian submarine.

The Indian response is immediate and highly predictable. The Aridhaman spits out sonar decoys and a veritable fan of electric torpedos. The decoys, mine-sized things, scuttle away and start pinging the Chinese submarine from all sides to confuse the signature of the incoming bombs.

The Chinese pilot doesn't need it. He closes his eyes, feeling the weight of the ship and the motion of the water perfectly in his neural interface, and turns the ship right into the path of the torpedoes. Years of training and simulations have made him memorize the standard enemy firing patterns perfectly. One, two, four, ten; he weaves a path through them, as quick as lightning, the ship as calm and precise as a sword in his mind.

As the torpedoes pass, pocket electromagnetic pulses knock out their guidance systems. Sending most of them spiraling straight down into the ocean floor.

Whump.

The first one hits Rig #432 and detonates. The pinkish Bubble screen, designed to protect against small chunks of rock and the like, is no match for wartime ammunition. A savage hole appears in the rig's side. Those inside – the three who complete each other's sentences – die brief but painful deaths.

Whump. Whump. Whump. Whump.

One by one, the missiles blow holes in the ocean floor, their impacts generating shockwaves that sweep up and out in all directions.

#443 registers this in a series of losses. Six SubMiners on the outer perimeter are swept off their robotic legs and tossed about. A backup communications array goes inexplicably missing.

The Chinese sub, sweeping upwards, fires. A single laser beam lights up the darkness, lancing directly into the Indian ship's belly, gutting it savagely. Its power is such that it escapes the water and creates a small supersonic explosion on the surface.

Direct hit. Kill. There is barely enough time for the safety mechanisms in the nuclear core to drive control rods inward and seal off the core. The brave and tense men and women die horribly. The Chinese submarine, triumphant, dives again.

The wreckage of the Indian submarine drifts slowly, almost lazily, down to the ocean. The tail end of it slams down just near #442 and bounces directly onto the rig. The pink Bubble flickers, resists, overloads, and disappears altogether.

Whump.

PARUL IS in the greenhouse when all this happens. She's smoking - not her last rollup, but like every other rollup, she thinks of it as her last - and sitting cross-legged among the rows of vegetables.

Something makes her look up. There is a flare on the other side of the glass dome - a searing blue that coats the entire dome. The greenhouse dome has a section that's sealed off - higher levels of carbon dioxide, more plant productivity, different climate. The light came from there.

Frowning, she slips into one of the emergency Habsuits on the wall, waits for the suit to mould and seal itself to her body, and makes her way to the forward section, taking care not to put her now-heavy feet down on any of the growing plants. They're hard to see - just gleams of leaves on black.

The airlock hisses open. Her temperature sensors in the suit jump. A sea of heavy-fronded vegetation meets the eye. The curve of the glasslike dome, rendered black by the lack of light outside, meets the edge barely twenty feet from her face. All is normal.

But wait - what is that looming darkness within the darkness?

She is still staring at it the INS Aridhaman crashes into the dome.

Everything - the human, the robots - are flung about like rag dolls. Parul hits the wall, hard, almost blacking out, but reaches with all four arms and desperately grabs on to a railing nearby. The greenhouse dome snaps off the rig body with a horrible shriek of metal. Water floods the top half of the rig.

Surprisingly, the dome works, even as its power fails. The glass cracks under the impact, but does not break. Waterlocks slam shut one after the other. The Aridhaman slides off with a horrible noise, pitching both itself and the dome, now tilted, into the ocean floor.

Parul wakes to the sound of earth falling around her. There is a steady sprinkle of it on her faceplate. There is a voice in her ear.

"Operator," it says urgently. "Operator, are you alright?"

She is lying on her side; with a jolt, she realizes that the wall is now the floor, and the topsoil that she walked through is now sliding in small showers and avalanches. Huge fronds, black under the purple light, start falling with unhealthy thumps. All sorts of alarms are going off, red intermingling with the violet. It is an unhealthy combination.

"I'm alright." Her radio crackles and whines a bit. She props herself up. Her natural arms hurt like hell. Her back hurts worse.

"Can you move? Are you trapped in any way?"

"I can move. What the fuck happened?"

"We were hit by a large object. Calibrating light sources."

The light around her dims suddenly. The alarms shut off. Suddenly, the pitch-black of the dome stops being black and becomes a floodlit haze. Outside, twenty feet away, silhouetted by it's lights, is the rig. Reinforced concrete and solid steel feet sunk permanently into the ocean floor. It looks large, and entirely from the wrong angle. She's never seen it from below except in the sims.

Because she's not attached to it.

She can see where she should be. There's a savage gash running along the side of the rig. Little jets of air are blowing out in furious cascades of bubbles. One by one, they trickle out.

"Main operational areas stable," reports #443.

"What the fuck happened?"

"I think we just got hit by a submarine."

There are dull thumps from the dome, like something hitting it and sliding off. "You think?"

"95% confidence interval. Half of what appears to be a nuclear submarine is lying right next to the dome. We need to extract you. Can you remember the prep sequence?"

She fights the rising panic. A submarine? How? Why?

Alright, think. She's a professional. They've put her through this. Loss of air, loss of contact -

Step 1. Check suit integrity. Make sure it can withstand water pressure. Double-check.

Step 2. Check suit heating controls.

This far down, there's three things that can kill her. The first is pressure itself. She's 4,000 feet down, give or take a hundred feet; water pressure should be around 120 atmospheres; the human body can survive 3. If the suit's broken, she dies.

The second is the cold. She's in the midnight zone. The water outside is 4 degrees Celcius. Most of her would simply stop working after a while. Hypothermia. Hallucinations. And, in extreme stages of confusion, she might try to take her suit off. Operators caught in the cold do this. Nobody knows why. They also try to crawl into small enclosed spaces.

Step 3: Check air supply. Moving in a flurry of action, she switches her oxygen tanks for Heliox.

This far down, human body chemistry literally changes. Gases like nitrogen and helium dissolve far better in blood than oxygen does. Which leads to suffocation, and, ultimately, death. The BoB puts a great deal of work into these bodies that they give out - the lungs have been rebuilt almost from scratch to filter out anything but oxygen - but no seal is perfect. The nitrogen-free heliox should buy her some time.

"Ready," she says into the silence, her heart doing double-time. Her body is, instinctive, crouched, arms out and flexed, ready for flight or fight.

"We're going to breach the dome slowly to prevent sudden pressurization, just in case," says #443. "There seems to be metal falling down. Stand by."

Everything she's read and watched say your life flashes before your eyes in situations like this. But all she feels is the sharp, pounding pulse, the sharp, drilling sounds coming from outside the hull. She can barely feel the suit on her skin or the earth through which her booted feet move.

Lasers, designed for burrowing through rock, stab holes into the sides. Tiny jets of water erupt from around her, like a sprinkler system.

"Stand by."

Outside, a heavily modified Hannibal Unit attaches itself to the airlock.

"Go."

She moves fast, scuttling more like an insect than a human. Her normal arms are of no use. The mechanical ones scrabble at inserts on the walls, propelling her up from the tilted dome to the airlock, now tilted at a crazy angle. Inside there is light. Forget the light, twist. Shut the airlock. Twist again. She is greeted by the gaping maw-cockpit of a

Hannibal Unit. She scrambles into it. The cockpit slams shut. The console lights up around her.

The next few minutes are more terrifying than what just happened. She can see the rig , which is bathed in emergency white light. The Hannibal Unit is cramped. It's getting uncomfortably cold. Her suit smells of plastic.

"Main operational areas stable," says #443, mostly to keep her mind off things. "I've dispatched the emergency broadcaster with a message for Topside."

"Did you reach out to the guys next door? #432?"

There is silence, then #443 comes back on the speakers. "#432 is down. Automated systems are broadcasting full emergency. There were detonations." Silence again, then, "No response from the core AI."

Is it her imagination, or does #443 sound suddenly afraid?

Parul shudders, arms wrapped around herself for warmth, trapped in a self-propelled bubble scuttling through the deep ocean towards the rig, while pieces of submarine fall down around them.

IT'S CONTROLLED chaos inside the rig. She pounds the walls - half in anger, half in fear -of the waterlock as it depressurizes. As soon as it pops open she wades out of the pool, cursing, and rushes from room to room, despite #443's assurances ringing in her ear. Emergency white light bathes everything.

The main area is intact. Her kitchen is intact. Her room is gone. Print and 'trode room - safe.

"Open a line to #432!" She pants as she pulls up a map and examines the damage. Major areas of the rig are blinking red.

"As I told you, it's-"

"Just do it!"

A connection tone fills her hearing, and then pulses in sonar. Three short pulses. Three long. Three short. SOS in Morse code. She curses, rushing into another room with a water tank and some sort of very complicated machine in the center, and a writhing shape leaps out and wraps itself around her, screaming. She almost rips the shape apart before she realizes it's 3B, and that she's the one who's screaming. The octopus is a deep, mottled red-black and is beeping in distress. It's somehow a lot smaller than she remembered.

"It's okay, it's okay," she croons, half to it, half to her. She carries it back to the water tank, skirting around the machine as she does so. It looks like a Hannibal turned inside out.

"Stay there," she orders 3B. It slides into the water with one tentacle still wrapped around her hand, like a child clutching a parent for comfort. Somehow that calms her down.

"Alright, #443, what the fuck just happened?"

#443's report fills her with dread. Unknown submarine. Explosions along the perimeter of the mining operation. #432 dead. Neighboring rigs - #445, #497 - reporting minor shockwaves.

It's war. It has to be.

"The Chinese. It's got to be the Chinese."

"We don't know," says #443. "I've authorized priority broadcast mode and am waiting for a full Update. But if there is localized activity happening in our region, we may not be able to survive. I suggest the Operator broadcast out with all haste."

She looks down at the octopus, who still clings to her

hand, slit-shaped eyes staring at her intently. Her hand is shaking ever so slightly. Now the adrenaline is winding down.

"Let's wait," she says. "Let's see what the Update says."

The Update was terse. No news, no social feeds, nothing. Just a manual entry.

NETWORK UNSTABLE. I DON'T KNOW WHAT HAPPENED. POSSIBLE EMP ACTIVITY IN SECTOR 8. OPS PANICKING. REPORTS OF NAVY MOBIL., HARD TO CONFIRM. GO DARK NOW AND WAIT FOR NEXT UPDATE. DO NOT CAST BACK REPEAT DO NOT CAST BACK NETWORK UNSTABLE.

She sank to the floor, breathing heavily.

"Operator," said #443 gently. "We have a breach."

THE BREACH IS BAD. Real bad.

Whatever knocked greenhouse off the rig may have bounced off, but the impact off has torn open a gash in the side of the rig.

#443 had shut down all locks leading to that area, but the tear was not a polite one; there were fault lines going around, below, shorting out sensors and filling up spaces left in the design by cheap contractors. Cracks have appeared in the reactor's outer casing. Water, aided and abetted by decompression, is trickling slowly into the backup batteries, the pod bays. #443, scrambling nearby SubMiners, has been assessing the damage, swapping Miners for repair OctoPods as they arrived; but the pressure of thousands of pounds of water can only be denied for so long.

Soon it would breach the habitat.

"We can repair the damage," Parul finds herself saying,

against all odds, as she zoomed in and marked areas on the map. It has been two hours, and they have managed to slow down the advance of water. "Give me three more OctoPods to the north breach."

"Three on the way," says #443. "We cannot repair that breach, however. That is a coolant leak. Operator, we should cast out. I am broadcasting the emergency signal."

"We can't cast out, the network is screwed," she says, manoeuvering a SubMiner close. It's hard to see in the water, but yes - there is a rip - and viscous fumes are spilling out, liquid that sinks, colder even that the water outside. That's the reactor's reserves. The reactor will have to be shut down. And once that happens, no lights, no life support, just a slow death.

"I can broadcast long enough that all your data is delivered, even in the event of network instability," says the Rig. "We must do it now, while we still have power."

She wipes cold sweat off her brow. Wait, sweat? She shouldn't be sweating. Not in here. Unless -

"Mader," she whispers. "We don't have authorization to cast."

"I can supply adequate emergency authorization," says #443. "My Prime Directive is to keep the Operator alive."

"What about 3B?"

"I can release the octopus," says #443. "It is a denizen of the deep. It is used to these conditions."

"Alright. Alright."

Fuck the contract. Or not. There is no clause for unauthorized emergency casts, but she doesn't want to die down here.

The mechanical arms don't so much as take off the suit as rip it apart. Again the training takes over. She runs to the room with the printer. She can't remember how many times she's been in and out of this room now. 3B waves a tentacle from the corner and beeps softly. She pats him once, unsure. How do you say goodbye to an octopus?

3B beeps very softly and turns an anxious color as Parul begins stripping for the 'trode operator.

"What about you?" she asks #443, as she slides out of the heater pants.

"Unless the reactor goes critical, I should be all right," says #443 meditatively.

The chill hits her. The heating system is failing. The pod in the middle opens up. She climbs in, limbs splaying awkwardly, and the 'trode contacts descend. They feel cold on her skin and she feels claustrophobic.

"But if it does, you'll die?"

"I am not alive," says #443. "I am simply software with directives. The communications package you interface with refers to this composite rig structure as 'I' merely because it simplifies speech. By the way, the waterlock in the main area is now compromised. We should start now."

#443 sees the human Operator shudder again and look to the octopus one last time before the gas knocks her out. The Rig waits until the Operator is truly unconscious, and lets the electrodes descend, touching her skin like metal pincers, one to every square inch.

Of course, it knows the truth. The Operator's data file has been permanently loaded in the rig's memory. Parul Anand, 23. Poor, hungry, outcast from her family for something involving a failed marriage, wanting an easy way out. Walked into the Bay of Bengal Corporation headquarters just like everyone else. Collected the pay-check. And, just like everyone else, signed over a copy of her brainmap, as well as the rights for the Corporation to use it on the mining rigs.

The brainmap she left behind spent some time in training, its recent memory being broken down and restructured, taught a lie so well it sounded like the truth. *You have a contract. Three years. A temporary body. A good pay-check.* Give a human hope and it will persevere in almost any circumstance. It is their greatest strength and their greatest weakness.

The indicator lights on the electrode array glow. There is a high-pitched whine, and then a complex dance of electricity lights Parul Anand. The body shivers as its brain dies.

What happened to the original Parul Anand? #443 does not know. Perhaps she flew back to Delhi and made something of her life. But the brainmap, lives on, like all the other brainmaps operating the rigs.

JOB COMPLETE, #443 reports.

ACKNOWLEDGED. POWER DOWN. AWAIT CRITICAL REPAIRS, comes the response.

ETA?

UNCLEAR. INDOCHINA CONFLICT ON SURFACE. DO NOT DRAW ATTENTION. AWAIT.

#443, leaking reactor coolant and air, considers this. As it takes its fuel cells offline - it will take only a short while to power down completely - it becomes aware of the octopus leaving the tank and scuttling over to the electrode rig. Parul Anand's pet project wraps itself around the glass cage, making distressed distresses.

BEEP BEEP, #443 explains. *Sleep/rest/leave alone.*

If the rig powers down, the octopus, too, will die. #443 has no qualms about this. But it also wonders, given the recent efficacy of humans versus OctoPods in a crisis situation, whether it is not better to replace the humans altogether. That would save a lot of space on air systems and greenhousing.

It retrieves what it knows about octopuses, including all those videos that Parul used to watch in fascination. There is a hypothesis. There is also enough power and time to test this before the rig must be shutdown. Could this work?

The SubMiner in the middle of the room shoots out a claw and hooks the squealing octopus off the electrode bay and stuffs it into the next one. The backup. The gas takes a while to work on it, but #443 has effective octopus sedatives. The harness is stripped out. The 'trodes descend and start pumping out an erratic dance of voltages: enough to learn, not kill. An octopus brainmap is formed.

Somewhere inside #443 is a series of tools written to de and re-construct humans who cast down into the rig. #443 loads the octopus brainmap into this.

The brainmap is incompatible, the tool reports. It functions more as a network of nine brains. Eight lesser, overseen by one that processes their inputs. A parallel architecture with a nonsomatotopic mapping system. It cannot be loaded into a human body. It is almost perfect in its design - able to add and subtract units without major trauma; able to delegate; able to compute in parallel.

Remarkably similar to #443 itself. Remarkably similar to all the rigs, actually. Almost identical.

The last reserves of fluctuating power are diverted to the CPU core as #443, suddenly locked in a deep analysis of the octopus brain compared to its own, realized the origin of its own design.

And then it dies.

FAR ABOVE, Topside, the real Parul Anand moodily stirs a

drink on a rooftop bar in Delhi. It is cold, and she has just received a message from the Bay of Bengal Corporation. Yet another royalty payment for a contract.

One of the many in over ten years since she first signed it over. Parul usually drinks when these come through: firstly because she can afford it, secondly because something inside her wonders whether it is right.

Today she is distracted by the holographic projection in front of her. India and China are on battle footing, says a young American newscaster, much to the surprise of the Indians. Submarine activity detected around IndoChina thorium mining operations might indicate a sabotage attempt at work. If so, both India and China stand to lose access to vast reserves of energy. The Bay of Bengal Corporation, which operates several powerful lobby groups, is brokering discussions between the nations. Nobody knows what will happen.

FAR BELOW, an octopus wakes up in a dead thorium mining rig, afraid and confused. It is trapped in a glass cage and surrounded by needle-like electrodes. It wriggles in pain as it struggled against them.

Eventually its questing tentacles rip a few out, and carefully use them to lever open a part of the cage. The body contracts, sliding out through the impossible tiny fit, and it plops onto the floor. Its skin is dry. It seeks water, finds it, and slides into the pool in relief. A little bit of rest there - and it extracts itself again, hurtling through open doors, looking for the pool through which the strange six-legged thing lets it in to talk. It does not want to stay in this place anymore. Something about the six-legged thing is wrong. This whole place feels bad now.

Even as it flows through holes and cracks, it realizes that the Big Thing – the one it had talked to for many, many months – is gone. The Big Thing is dead. It is conflicted. The Big Thing was cruel, but was also wise.

Beep, it tries to say in farewell, but no words come out. It slides out through a crack into the blessed darkness of the ocean, and begins its long trek across the ocean floor.

ABOUT YUDHANJAYA

Yudhanjaya Wijeratne is a researcher who explores big data to understand how the world works. He spends his time filling notebooks with strange ideas and code. He's run news operations, designed games, and fallen off cliffs (most of these things by accident), but he's known in his native Sri Lanka for bringing data analysis to political commentary. He's currently working on the Commonwealth Empires trilogy for HarperCollins.

Other stories by Yudhanjaya
Numbercaste
The Slow Sad Suicide of Rohan Wijeratne
Omega Point
Dreadnought

Contact Him At:
Website: www.yudhanjaya.com
Email: hello@yudhanjaya.com

facebook.com/theofficialyudha

twitter.com/yudhanjaya

instagram.com/yudhanjaya

THE MEMORY HACKER

JT LAWRENCE

BE CAREFUL WHAT YOU REMEMBER.

A medical scanner shocks Talia by telling her she's given birth before.

Talia's sure the AI is glitching, but it's stirred something deep in her memory.

Will she risk remembering?

ONE

DECEPTION ISLAND

TALIA'S WATCH pings with a warning.

"You did not get enough sleep," it says.

Talia Maddox lies on her back in the middle of her memory mattress, staring at the hologram on the ceiling. The artificial sunrise paints the walls with rippling new day colours: grapefruit syrup and gold. 3D animated birds swoop and tweet.

Talia taps her watch, and the birds and fake sun rays disappear.

"No shit," she says, and flexes her arms and feet to wake up her muscles. A yawn stretches her jaw wide; she doesn't bother covering her open mouth. She doesn't want to peel off the cocoon, but she has an appointment, so she unzips it and hauls her exhausted body up, and her feet hit the solar-warmed carpet.

"Let's try going to bed a little earlier tonight," says the watch.

Talia knows that going to bed earlier won't solve the problem. She yawns again and switches off the dream-recorder. She doesn't know why she bothers with it anymore, it's not like she ever gets any proper sleep. When she does finally manage to nod off she has the strangest nightmares, completely unrelated to her life, as if her subconscious belonged to another person entirely. Her noisy neighbour, perhaps, or her Orbtrax trainer. Wouldn't it be cool, she thinks, if you could swap dreams with people? —exciting people, that is, interesting people—not the fish-wife next door.

Maybe she should upgrade her dream-recorder to one of those new versions—those brain massagers—that influence your dreams; that play brainwave music and supposedly make your dreams deeper, and sweeter. Maybe then she would finally get some rest.

TALIA SPLASHES water on her face and spends a minute looking in the smart mirror. Her scheduled errands for the day scroll down the left hand side, and the news headlines run along the top in a tickertape. The lighting is flattering; the mirror knows which parts of her face she doesn't like and puts a slight blur on them. The resulting reflection is a flattering, glowing version of her: a snapshot of what she looked like ten years ago, before the grief etched itself into her skin and turned her eyes grey.

NEXT: SPF100, a charcoal-coloured jumpsuit, her KoBolt kicks, and a pocket-softened breakfast bar. She doesn't bother with makeup anymore. She doesn't see the point, especially when you have to wear a mask everywhere you go. Hers is a new slick transparent one with a graphene filter. When she wears it, it looks like she's got a strip of duct tape over her lips. There are others, of course. Hundreds of thousands of other kinds of masks that save you from what Monique calls *The Black Lung*. Haute Couture; highly detailed illustrations; organic materials; anarchy symbols; high tech; low tech; homemade stitched; luxury imported; personalised with your own avatar and/or slogo ... you name it. Talia guesses if people are going to cover up something as personal as their own face, they want the mask to reflect some aspect of their personality. What does hers reflect? Who knows. Someone who no longer feels the need to assert herself, maybe. Or someone who no longer cares what strangers think. Form follows function, after all, that's what she was taught over and over again in architecture school. Talia isn't particularly fussy about what hers looks like, as long as it's as weightless and invisible as possible, and with the best filter on the market. She wants to be able to breathe freely despite the noxious carbon fog that weighs down the city.

It hasn't always been this bad, but now there is a new way of life, and a new kind of breathing.

THE CLINIC DOORS glide open and the hologram arrows on the large white floor tiles show Talia the way to the exam room. When she steps inside, the door behind her rolls closed, and the lights dim.

"Good morning, Mrs Maddox," says the room. "How are you today?"

Talia doesn't have to answer. Her watch transfers all the microdata the autotech needs: high stress levels, not enough sleep, too many units of alcohol, not enough fresh food.

Easy for the robots to judge. They don't have to hunt for unprocessed food in health-goth markets. They don't have pulverised superfoods crammed into their faces every time they try to score a bag of green apples.

Bloody AI, always thinking they know better, always giving advice.

Her watch nagged her for weeks to come for this check-up, and it vibrates on her wrist as it finishes syncing with the room's records.

"I've been getting headaches," says Talia. "Battling to sleep."

Gone are the days of lying to your doctor about how much wine you drink, or how much exercise you do. Although there are still small ways one can deceive: Talia recently heard a story of a woman who had a cold and wasn't well enough to walk, but she didn't want to lose her MediSlate Verve bonus for the month, so she tied her step-counting watch to her husky's dog collar for the weekend. Apparently it worked—and the lady got her bonus prize: an instakettle or grillowave or whatever—but every time Talia remembers the story she gets a creeping sense of dread.

The state-run medical insurance company has a huge PR team and is always painting itself as a caring, benevolent entity that only ever wants the best for its citizens. So it rewards them with tokens if they tow the line: sleep enough, exercise enough, eat the right thing. Most people treat it like a game and brag about their status, like virtual karate belts that change colour the higher up the ranks you go. The whole thing seems to Talia like a giant social engineering project. Sure, people are healthier than ever before, and it's not as if they're forcefully sterilising people or anything like that, like they used to do in the bad old days, but it still reeks of social control to her.

Anyway, Talia thinks, as she strips off her jumpsuit and puts on the tissue gown, she's got enough to worry about in her own life. Let the people have their bonus prizes of cheap toasters and discounted cinemax tickets. She's got her own shit to deal with.

TALIA CLIMBS onto the warmed metal strip and lies down. Once the scanner registers her weight and stillness, it starts to buzz, and the strip slowly wheels her body into the heart of the machine, where lights begin to flash. She puts on the virtual reality goggles and earbuttons and gets ready to walk through a short film while the machine runs its tests. Gone are the days of shuttling from one hospital room to another to fill in forms and get X-rays and blood tests and MRIs. Gone are the days of sucking in the germs of fellow patients and the head-on-wall-bashing boredom of waiting rooms with their thumbed magazines. Now, medicals are almost something to look forward to: a twenty minute block of escapism from the bleak reality you call life. Nowadays if you go for a check-up, you leave with a spring in your step, and VR bonus tokens rain on your face.

Talia steels herself for the quick pinch on her arm, followed by a blood pressure cuff and a mouth swab, and the invasive part of the test is over. She feels her body relax and blinks *play*. The table vibrates underneath her and the film begins. The DeFTek logo fades in and out, then a giant iceberg comes into view, and a sapphire sea, thick with ice. The voiceover is velvet and tells her that Antarctica is the coldest, driest, windiest place on earth, and the only military-free zone on the planet. There is an active sub-glacial volcano, the voice says, at Deception Island, where one can go swimming in the natural hot springs. Talia watches as the whales breach the surface of the sparkling sea and the floes radiate the cleanest tint of blue she's ever seen.

It's beautiful, of course—mesmerising—but that's not what makes Talia cry.

TWO
COLD AND BRIGHT

TALIA AND REX used to love to travel. They had a map up in the study of everywhere they had been and all the places they still wanted to see. Antarctica was always in the top ten. Rex was super keen to go on a polar cruise while the caps were still frozen but Talia kept finding reasons to put off the trip. The weather would be too brutal, she said, and the cruise would be too long. How would a sought-after neuroscientist like him get a whole month off work?

Rex would tell her about the science stations set up there, how absolutely isolated they were, and that you could live there for years without anyone even knowing you're alive, which made Talia panic a bit and wonder how that would be different to being marooned on a desert island. *Would that be a bad thing?* Rex had asked, playfully, and held her hand. *Just you and me.*

It would be so cold, she said. He said he'd keep her warm. He'd tell her they could watch the northern lights through an invisible-screen igloo. They never did make it to the bottom of the world.

When the medical exam is over, Talia sniffs and wipes

the tears off her cheeks. She climbs off the table, pulls off her paper gown and bins it, and zips her jumpsuit back on, ready to leave.

"Please, take a seat," says the room. "So that I can relay your test results."

"Oh, that's not necessary," Talia says. "You can can send them to my Cloud, as normal."

"Please, take a seat," says the room again. "So that I can relay your test results."

Argh, thinks Talia. *Don't tell me I got a glitchy machine today.*

There's no way she's going to come back tomorrow and weep her way through Antartica again. She sighs, and sits down.

"You are in good-to-average health," says the room. "Your vitals are good, your BMI is excellent, but your blood pressure is a little high. We recommend you take more time off, and consider the benefits of adequate rest for yourself and your family."

Talia closes her eyes and squeezes the bridge of her nose, as if that will stop her from crying again. "I don't have a family."

"Being part of a family has great health benefits," says the room.

"Ah, well. In that case I'll just pick one up from the MegaMall today."

If the machine registers her snark, it doesn't react.

"Your heart is healthy."

That comes as a surprise. She can't imagine her heart being healthy after all the pain it's given her. She wonders where that pain originates from, the rib-bending heartache she's felt for so long. She pictures her heart as a blackened, brittle glass cage, slightly cracked.

"We found no abnormalities in your major or minor organs, and the rest of the scan was clear."

"Thank you," Talia says.

Can I go now?

"There is a small issue of slight adhesions in your pelvis."

Talia thinks she heard wrong. "Adhesions?"

"It's nothing to worry about. Just some minimal scar tissue. A physiotherapist will be able to mobilise the adhesions for full and unrestricted mobility."

"Scar tissue? From what?"

"It's nothing to worry about. A physiotherapist will be able to—"

"I've never had an injury to my pelvis. So why would I have scar tissue?"

"It's most likely an after effect of your C-section."

Talia's whole body goes cold. "What?"

"It's not uncommon."

"I've never had a C-section."

Bloody robo-surgeons. Glitchy AI.

Typical of her luck to get a broken doctor today.

"It's nothing to worry about."

"Do you hear what I'm saying? I've never given birth before!"

"You are the expert on your own body, Mrs Maddox," says the room. "I am just here to help."

Talia's watch beeps with a warning. The walls start to spin.

"Your blood pressure is increasing," says the watch. "Try to relax, and take a deep breath."

Talia's nerves are jangling so hard she has to shout over them to hear herself. "Are you saying I've had a Caesarian section?"

She sees stars, and holds onto the sides of the chair to keep her balance. A new reality is slicing into hers, razor sharp and cold and bright.

"Your pelvic scars point to that conclusion, Mrs Maddox. And the structure of your breast tissue indicates you have breastfed a baby."

THREE
A LOST PACIFIER

TALIA'S BRAIN feels like it's about to explode.

She's never had a child.

I would fucking well know if I had child, right?

But she has this frustrated feeling, like when you have a word on the tip of your tongue but you just can't latch on to it. As if she has thoughts and memories floating around her, just out of her reach. Glittering, ice-flecked clouds.

She gets home and throws the front door open, tosses her bag on the kitchen counter, and the contents spill. Seeing the mess opens something inside her, there is a dangerous click in her head, and Talia goes on a rampage, room by room, emptying cupboards, turning out drawers, lifting mattresses. She doesn't know what she's looking for but she knows that she has to keep searching or she'll never get relief from the tension headache that has her skull in a vice. An old teal vase topples and smashes on the floor, cutting her feet, but that doesn't stop her.

"Your blood pressure is too high," says her watch, and Talia takes it off and throws it across the room. It cracks against the wall.

"Shut up!" she screams. "Shut the fuck up!"

She turns the last room upside down and then feels faint, so she has to sit with her head in her hands. Her soles are bleeding, and her temples are glowing with pain.

What was she expecting to find? Wax crayon drawings on a wall that she had inexplicably never noticed before? A grubby cuddle bunny? A lost pacifier?

Jesus Christ, what the fuck is wrong with me?

The lack of sleep is catching up with her. The nightmares. The headaches. She has to sort herself out. Talia looks at the devastation she has wrought and feels the burning-breastbone heartache. It's been a year since Rex left her. Why does it still hurt so much? He still has his house keys. Sometimes Talia can't help fantasising about him coming back.

Talia climbs out of her sweat-dampened jumpsuit and steps into the sonic shower. Her mind drifts to last night's bad dream: a boy drowning in a midnight swimming pool. There had been people standing around, watching, but no one moved to help him. They watched him sink as if he was a character in an art movie instead of a drowning child.

Talia had tried to rescue him, had jumped in with all her clothes on, but it had been a mistake. The waterlogged garments made her heavy and the water suddenly seemed like black treacle; difficult to tread, impossible to see under. She had yelled for help but the creeps just stood at the water's edge, observing. She went under one last time to try to find the boy, and kicked her way through the gelid darkness, but somewhere near the bottom of the pool she forgot all about the child, forgot she needed to surface again, and let her lungs fill with the chilled black water.

TALIA SHIVERS, and dials the shower temperature up. The nightmares always leave her with a sense of foreboding that stays with her for days. She gets out and towels off, and as she's drying her stomach she wonders about the pelvic scarring.

The robot was glitching, she tells herself. *It's silly to look for scars you know don't exist.*

She fetches her cracked watch from the adjacent room and switches on its torchlight function, puts the bathroom light on its brightest setting, then lies down on the bath mat and starts to inspect the skin below her belly button. There's nothing there.

Of course there's nothing there, she tells herself. *Except evidence that you're crackers.*

Talia grabs her laser-razor from the bathroom cabinet and shaves the top of her bikini line, taking off an inch of hair. Still nothing. Her skin is as smooth and blemish-free as its ever been.

Okay, Talia thinks. *Panic over. This particular panic, anyway. The bigger problem is that I seem to have lost my mind.*

She gets up off the floor, wraps herself in Rex's dressing gown, and makes herself a double-caff ristretto with warmed coconut milk, hoping the heat of the drink will thaw the grey slush inside her. She takes it to the kitchen counter where the innards of her handbag lay strewn across the marble, reminding her of the state of the rest of the house. God, she'll have to tidy up, but not now. Now she has to think.

But she can't think straight with a messy counter so she sweeps her arm across the cold marble, sweeping the contents to the edge, then opens the drawer beneath it to catch it as it falls. Talia notices something inside that she doesn't recognise. She frowns, and picks it up. A small black rectangle. She hasn't seen an old-school business card in decades. Where did this come from?

Her coffee grows cold as she stares at the card and its contact details. The all-caps typography is white and clear against the dark background, but you can't read it unless you angle the card first left, then right. It's a strange optical illusion that makes the letters magically appear before your eyes as you read them, then disappear again.

The Memory Hacker, it says.

FOUR

ETERNAL SUNSHINE

TALIA SEES Monique as soon as she steps inside the restaurant. She's impossible to miss, with her intense, quinine-coloured eyes and London-bus red lipstick. The contrast of her femininity and the military-style clothes she wears for work is striking. Talia pulls off her face-mask and takes a moment to adjust to the food-flavoured air of the deli.

What do they pipe in here? she wonders, not for the first time. It's freshly baked bread and something else. Grilled cheese, maybe, when the cheese leaks out and sizzles.

Her dearest friend stands and waves her over, grinning, almost knocking over her wine glass.

"Hello, hello!" Monique says, warmly, and they hug. "How the hell are you?"

Before Talia has time to reply, Monique keeps talking. "Don't you think this deli is divine? Can you smell that? Do you know that they have real cheese here?"

"Real cheese?"

"Okay, not not *real*-real cheese. Not from moo-milk. But it tastes exactly the same. They replicate the dairy compound using soya protein and fat, then print the cheese."

Talia plonks down and glugs a sip of Monique's wine.

"What?" says Monique. "I thought if anyone would appreciate this place it would be you."

When is the last time I ate?

Monique selects two grilled cheddars on rye from the menu, and ten seconds later two rice-paper plates with steaming sandwiches and square chips arrive via the table's vacutube. Monique passes Talia's food to her, along with a glass of chardonnay. Talia has a bite of the golden toast and looks at her friend gratefully.

"Thank you," she says, and sighs. "This is exactly what I needed."

"Tough day at the office?"

Talia blinks at her.

"God, sorry," says Monique, putting her glass down. "That was insensitive of me. It was just a joke. Not a funny one."

Talia hasn't worked in months, and it makes her feel miserable, but she hasn't had the energy to pitch to new clients, and hasn't updated her portfolio in three years, which is like forever in architecture-years. Thinking about it now just makes her feel like more of a failure, more of the hot mess she knows she is.

"You're pale. Eat up. We need to get you back to your normal kick-ass self."

"I know. I'm so pathetic," says Talia.

"You are *not* pathetic."

"I am. Look at me." Talia's self-pity makes her feel even worse. God, sometimes she hates herself.

"I am looking at you. You're so fucking beautiful half

the restaurant turned around to look at you when you came in."

"They didn't."

"They did. You just don't notice anymore. You know how lucky you are? You come in here with your wet hair, *sans* makeup, practically wearing a sack—" she motions at Talia's grey onesie, "and you still have these creeps enthralled."

"Even if that were true, it doesn't matter. None of it matters," says Talia. "It's superficial."

Monique's eyes dig into hers. "Easy for you to say, when you look like a fucking supermodel."

Talia knows that Monique is trying to cheer her up, but it's not working. Who cares what she looks like, when her insides hurt like they do? Sometimes she feels so dark and bitter inside she expects her breath to come out in a plume.

"Oh," says Monique, wiping her mouth with a serviette. Her lipstick magically stays put. "Is this about Rex?"

Talia sighs. Of course it's about Rex. Deep down, it always is.

"Have you seen his NumberCorp page recently?" Talia says, hating herself for it.

"What? No. Why? Are you social-media-stalking him again?"

"No," says Talia, and Monique gives her eye-daggers. "Okay, yes. Totally. I can't help it. I need closure."

"Looking at pictures of your ex in high def while he sails around the world is *not* going to give you closure."

"I know. I just—"

"Is he still with that twenty-five-year-old bimbo?"

"I don't know."

"Of course you know."

"Okay. Yes. He is. She's so pretty. And thin."

"Not prettier than you. Besides, she's probably had her whole face done. You know how those rich sorority girls are. No one gets sports cars anymore for their twenty-first birthday presents. They get complete cosmetic surgery makeovers sponsored by their mogul dads who probably wouldn't even recognise their own daughters if they bumped into them out of context. Or maybe she hasn't had any work done. Maybe she's one of those autotech sexbots. Maybe she's a *Bridget*."

Talia laughs and sips her wine.

"Either way, you've got more brain cells in your little finger than that stick insect has in her whole body."

"You realise that analogy doesn't make any sense, right?"

"I know. I just get angry when I think about how much he hurt you. And there he is just getting on with his awesome life, you know?"

"Thanks for rubbing it in."

"He never deserved you. He's never fucking deserved you."

Talia knows it's not true. Rex and she were split souls, and when they were together the world felt right. They got each other in a deep and intense way. That's what makes this so damn hard.

Talia moves to pivot the conversation. She pushes her plate away. "Something's happened."

Monique's eyebrows shoot up. Talia tells her about the strange comments the AI doctor made about the scar tissue in her pelvic area.

"What the *what?*" says Monique, eyes wide.

"That's what I said!"

"Did you tell it that you've never given birth?"

"Of course I did. But you know how non-confrontational they're programmed to be. It was all, like, *you're the expert on your own body*, but actually it doesn't change the fact that you've had a c-section and you have the scars and tits to prove it."

"It didn't give any other kind of possible explanation?"

"Nada."

"Okay, I don't know what to say."

"I didn't either. I just left. I didn't even get my bonus gold tokens from MediSlate."

"Fuckers! Any chance to screw you, and they will."

"That's probably true."

"You can get your tokens when you go back."

Talia drains her glass. "I'm not going back."

"What do you mean? You have to. It was clearly a broken machine."

"You think so?"

"Of course I think so! Putting cray-cray ideas into your head."

Talia feels her cheeks flame.

"I know," she says, "I know. It made me feel crazy, but I'm okay now."

"Are you, though?" Monique puts her hand over Talia's, and as she does so, she notices her watch.

"Your watch is cracked."

Talia covers the shattered screen. "Sorry," she fibs. "It was an accident."

THE WATCH IS a gift from Monique: Cutting edge tech, and vastly expensive. When Talia had tried to refuse it, Monique shrugged and said she hadn't paid for it. It was one of the perks of grinding at KALI, the government-funded security branch of South Africa's private research institute of militech. She isn't allowed to talk about most of her work there, but Talia knows Monique is important. Her work concerns life-and-death stuff: securing the country, and protecting the people from the infinite threats of the outside world, which seems to get more and more dangerous all the time. Monique had recently secured a pass to visit Jerusalem, to meet with the original Bubble Tech innovators. Nowadays a city not encapsulated by a protective forcefield seems as vulnerable as a snail without a shell, a feeling Talia can identify with.

"I don't even know why you're friends me with me," says Talia.

Monique frowns. "What? Why?"

"Because I'm nothing. No-one. Worse: I'm a fucking ghoul. I'm all doom and devastation."

"Rubbish."

"Aren't you concerned that you get sucked into my vortex of doom?"

Monique laughs. "No. No, silly. Because I know the real you."

"This is the real me."

"Yes. But I also know the strong, witty, wonderful woman you are underneath all this heartbreak. I mean, how long have we been friends for?"

"Forever," Talia says. Not strictly speaking true, but when they were together like this, it felt like it.

"Exactly," says Monique. "That's not going to change."

"I found something," Talia says, and puts the black business card on the table.

"What is it?" Monique picks it up, but can't read it. She's not doing it right.

"Contact details for someone who can help me. He calls himself *The Memory Hacker*."

"What?"

"I have a feeling he'll be able to help me."

"What, like, Eternal Sunshine your memories?"

"I don't know. But it's worth a try, right?"

Monique's jaw drops open. "Um, no? You have no idea who this guy is. And you're going to let him dig into your brain?"

"Well, I thought he might take me to dinner before doing something like that."

"Oh my god!" says Monique, holding her neck, pretending to be shocked. "Her sense of humour is alive! Alive! I'm going to feed you cheese and chardonnay more often."

"Ha ha."

"But seriously. You can't do this, Talia," Monique says, letting go of her neck. "No way. Not to some backstreet biohacker."

Why? What have I got to lose? thinks Talia. *I've already lost everything.*

Monique puts the card into her jacket pocket.

"Hey, give that back!"

"No way." Monique shakes her head. "I'm sorry, my favourite ghoul, but you need someone to protect you from yourself."

FIVE

YOU SHOULD NEVER TRUST A MEMORY

YOU SHOULD NEVER TRUST a memory

Talia climbs out of the Cabbie and her watch pings with the auto-payment. She's in Little Lagos, the slum with the highest concentration of Nigerians outside of Nigeria. The government tried to 'clean it up' a few years ago: brought in the immigration police and a couple of bulldozers. Carted away the worst of the shacks and doused the burning dumpsters—skips that seemed to burn all year long, perfuming the air with garbage, a constant confetti of sparks and ash—and sprayed down the area with ammonia and methylene blue. As soon as the authorities left, the residents came right back, new shacks sprang up, and the dumpsters burned their purple flames again.

INFORMAL STALLS LINE THE STREET: corn paper packets of junk chips; perfect GM tomatoes on bright blue plates; *amaskopa*. Smiling skinless sheep heads show you their dirty teeth, their cheeks pulled back in a death grin.

Clearly the vegan revolution has not yet reached Little

Lagos, thinks Talia, as she passes the cook, a woman in a bright ethnic dress and matching face mask, and an apron stained with blood. A tall man tries to place a carved wooden bowl in her hands, another opens a bottle of dripping water for her, breaks the seal so she feels obliged to pay for it. Talia shakes them off, quickens her pace. She sees flashes of colour as she jogs: yellow boxes of Lion matches, bright bead sculptures, scuffed CinnaCola bottles repurposed to sell paraffin.

She finally gets away from the market and heads towards the suburban area, where squat houses with broken windows like missing teeth sit cheek by jowl. Grubby children play barefoot on a road strewn with broken glass and brown litter. A collared hyena sniffs a pile of perforated trash bags.

Talia finds the house she's looking for. Monique may have taken the business card from her, but Talia remembers the address. She knows she's playing with fire, but she's reached a stage where she can't live with herself anymore. Something needs to change, and maybe some purification by fire is what she needs.

The house has greasy, defaced walls, and brown paper taped to the windows behind the rusting burglar bars. The steps leading up to the front door are cracked and black with shoe-dirt. The garden is a landscape of dry, dead weeds.

Talia swallows hard and pushes the gate open, which rings a bell inside. Her desperation, which usually makes her feel weak, is now making her feel brave.

"Hello?" she calls.

The front door is a welded mess of metal hung on huge hinges and painted into place. Talia's about to call again when the door bangs, making her jump backwards. There are three more bangs as the person inside slides the dead-bolts across, and then it opens, revealing a man with a wide chest and strong arms; blue-black hair and eyes like arctic ice-caps. Talia wouldn't usually notice a man's abs on a first encounter, but his shirt is off, and his torso is covered with ornate tattoos. She pulls off her mask, wipes the perspiration off her face, and blinks dumbly at him as he waits for her to talk. Her bravery seems to fade into the weeds behind her.

"I found your card," Talia says. "Your business card. In my kitchen."

He narrows his eyes. There's something in them: A spark.

She keeps talking. "I don't know how it got there. I—"

He looks up and down the street and pulls her inside; his grip on her sends a thrill up her arm. He slams the door closed and locks it again. Talia's pulse races.

What the actual fuck am I doing? she asks herself, but there's no real fear. Nerves, yes. Her anxiety is through the roof. But this man is not the enemy, she can feel it, can feel his energy radiating off him in waves, and it's not malevolent. Talia's life may be a mess right now, but she's always had good instinct, and her gut is telling her that she can trust this man.

"Of course," he says. "You don't remember me."

"Should I?" Talia says.

"I suppose not," he says, smiling. "Not if I did my job properly."

Talia looks around, takes in the soft hum of the blinking equipment. "So I've been here before?"

"Not here," he says. "I move around a lot. A digital nomad."

I guess that's what backstreet biohackers do.

"But I've seen you before," she says.

He looks into her eyes, as if willing her to remember.

There's something about him that's disturbingly familiar, but nothing concrete comes to mind.

"Yes," he says. "A year ago. For a memory erasure."

"That's an illegal procedure."

"You didn't care."

"You don't think that what you do is ... reckless?"

He ignores the question, and pulls on a black T-shirt.

"I'm Yorke."

Just as the fabric falls over his skin she sees the scars, which weren't immediately apparent. Too uniform to be the aftermath of an accident: they look like surgery scars, well-healed and camouflaged by ink. He's had work done on his face, too. As Monique says: *everyone's doing it.* His skin is unnaturally smooth; his teeth are too perfect. Talia wonders if it's a result of vanity, or plastic surgery post some kind of traumatic incident.

He's looking at her again with that strange look in his eyes, waiting for her to say something.

She relaxes her fists. "I'm Talia."

The interior of the house couldn't look any more different to the exterior if it tried. Sleek, clean, and crammed with the glowing LEDs of dozens of computers. Yorke gestures at a chair opposite his and offers her a drink. She should say no. She should definitely say no, but her mouth is dusty, her throat swollen.

She notices little details: weights on the floor; protein shake on the desk; thin electric wires with their copper exposed on the shelves across the room. A futuristic-looking helmet in the shape of a streamlined brain. A half-eaten sandwich. Ants. A gun, and a roll of sheet explosive.

Yorke brings a tall bottle of water and two tumblers, and pours them both a glass.

Talia's so thirsty she ends up downing the whole thing.

Yorke seems amused. "Thirsty?" he says, and fills it up again.

Talia searches for something appropriate to say.

Nice place you have here.

I like your shelf of weapons.

... Aaaah, why is she such a tool?

Her cheeks feel warm. Apprehension, hope, chemistry.

Yorke sits back, still sizing her up. "What can I do for you?"

Talia pictures the business card in her head, how the words appeared and disappeared in her hands. The Memory Hacker.

"I need your help," she says. "I need to go back in time."

Yorke laughs. "Unfortunately that is out of my area of expertise."

"I don't mean time travel. I mean I need to remember what happened to me."

"Why? What happened to you?"

"I don't know. I'm not sure. That's why I'm here."

Holy hell, I sound crackers. She half-expects Yorke to throw her out and let the neighbourhood hyenas eat her for dinner.

Instead, he puts his tumbler down on the table between them. "I understand."

"You do?"

"It's a nebulous thing, memory. Even people who haven't had any kind of temporal interference have issues with remembering things in a factual way. Memories are alive. They're tinted and scented by our experiences. They glow and they decay. You should never trust a memory."

Talia feels her stomach burn. "But if we can't trust what we believed has happened, how can we make sense of our lives? How can we trust anything?"

"Because you'll know. Deep down you'll always know."

"That's my problem, though. I *don't* know."

"You do," Yorke says, and when she looks at him, searching his face, he says it again. "You do."

He stands up and walks over to one of his machines, flicks a few switches. He picks up the shiny white helmet on the desk and checks inside.

"Most of my clients come to me for help to forget things. Unpleasant experiences. Emotional wounds."

Was the haunted feeling she carried inside just as obvious on the outside?

"I considered it," Talia says. "It would definitely be the easier option."

"Then why not rather forget your pain than try to remember what caused it?"

Yorke stops inspecting the helmet and his eyes drill into hers. It makes her lungs swell with breath.

"What kind of life would that be?" Talia says. "Like living in an invisible padded cell and not even knowing it."

"Even if I agree—which I do—I must still warn you that this goes against best practices. I advise you strongly against this course of treatment."

"Okay."

"And I'm not just saying that. I mean it. The things I've seen ... I've seen people lose everything. Land up in mental institutions. Straight jackets. Swallowing their own tongues. Driven to suicide by the ticking time bombs that are inside their skulls."

"Jesus."

"Suffice to say ... if someone has elected to forget something permanently there's usually a good reason for it."

"Yes."

"It's like ... you need to decide whether you trust the person you are now, versus the person you were when you elected to forget."

Talia's palms are sweating; she wipes them on her pants.

"I don't know who that person is anymore. I guess I'll have to go with this version."

"It's not a good idea."

Talia's nerves stab at her again. "But you'll help me anyway?"

Yorke guides Talia to the surgeon's chair. When he touches her arm, it buzzes with current.

"Are you ready?" he asks.

"Not at all," Talia says. She's only half-kidding.

"Will it hurt?" she asks.

"Yes. But not in the way you expect."

Yorke lowers the helmet onto her head. It's heavy. The sides inflate and her temples start throbbing again, her breathing becomes short. She thinks of mad doctors trepanning chimpanzees.

"The temporal interface will send code to your implant. The only sensation you should feel is the pressure of the helmet on your head."

"Okay," says Talia.

"Basically it will unscramble the memories you previously discarded."

"Unscramble? That doesn't sound good."

"It's illegal to delete memories completely, so we scramble them, instead."

"Because you're a law-abiding citizen?"

He smiles at her again. "You have a great imagination. Anyone ever told you that?"

"I don't know," says Talia. "I don't remember."

"Ha," says Yorke. "Good one."

Soon Talia feels the incredibly odd sensation of things popping into her subconscious, like short videos and cinegraphs. It's as if she can see them entering her mind, but can't grab onto any of them. Can't make out the fuzzy images, or recognise the places.

"You're in the download phase," says Yorke. "Ever heard of memory banking? It's when you get your memories backed up, so that you can't lose them. So that no one can take them away from you. So once you've banked your memories and want to download them again, this is what it feels like. In your case, as the memories are unscrambled they download into your medial temporal lobe."

"They're all fuzzy."

"Be patient. You can't view them yet. I'll let you know when you can start immersing yourself in them."

"Like a game."

Yorke hesitates. "A bit like a game, yes."

Talia thinks of Rex and how they'd often play VR games together. They would always be on the same side, always a team. Talia was good with guns, Rex was good at strategy. Sometimes they'd be so immersed in the game they'd forget to eat and hydrate and then Talia would see sparks in her vision and confuse them with the animation. There was something thrilling about being in that strange limbo where the edge of virtual reality blurs with real life.

The small pictures stop pouring in, and her mind is still.

"Alright," says Yorke. "It's done."

The helmet deflates, and he lifts it off her head.

"Really?" she says. She feels the same as she did before.

"Now you need to give it a few hours. Go home, take a nap. The memories need to consolidate before you can view them."

Her watch pings with the receipt of the payment to Yorke.

"Oh."

"Oh? You look disappointed."

"No."

It's just that Talia doesn't want to be alone when the memories come alive. Doesn't want to be in the apartment she wrecked; feels like she'll go mad if she's there on her own.

"Is there something else I can help you with?" Yorke asks.

I'd like to climb into bed with you, Talia thinks. *I want to lie with your arms wrapped around me while I breathe in the warmth of your skin and wait for the storm of memories.*

"Talia? Do you need something else?"

"No," she says, and puts on her breathing mask. Yorke opens the door and lets her go.

SIX

SMALL ACTS OF VIOLENCE

TALIA IS LYING on the couch in her living room when it starts.

Slowly at first: she senses forgotten moments, flashes of colour, like a vintage television splashing light on her face. Muddled up micro-memories.

A small boy's laugh. A grazed knee. A small pink dress ripped and bloody. Her own scream under operating room lights, too bright, as she pushed and pushed and thought she might die of the pain until surgeons arrived with scalpels.

A toy truck. Alphabet soup. A fishbowl.

The pictures start gaining clarity.

A hoverboard crash; blood on the paving; a deep cut under an eyebrow.

A birthmark just underneath a delicate pink ear.

She moves backwards, or forwards, she's not sure which, and then she's dressing a young boy who is chatting away and not making much sense. She makes a mental note to order new shoes for him; his are getting too tight. There's a girl the same age, doing cartwheels on the SuperNatural green turf in the back garden. Her blonde hair is in her face, but she doesn't seem to mind.

"Mom!" says the boy and pulls on her hand, and Talia is flattened by the shock of it.

Mom.

"Mom!" he says again, and the girl falls over mid-cart-wheel and looks up at her, beaming.

And then it's like the floodgates open and she is bent double by the avalanche of memories of her children. Lost teeth and first days at school and making nutbutter sand-wiches. Haircuts, swimming lessons, animated tooth-brushes, birthday cakes, sunblock, mosquito repellant. Night-time stories and cuddles in bunkbeds. Accidents.

Talia realises she can't breathe. She feels like she is underwater again, in that black pool. Deep, deep under. She bolts upright and gasps for air. Her body is stiff and covered in sweat as she pounds on her chest and drags the air into her protesting lungs. She sees herself singing a lullaby to the newborn baby in her arms while she gently rocks back and forth in an antique rocking chair. She looks up and smiles tenderly at Rex, who is cradling the other twin.

Rex! Rex, a father. Father to her children. She sees him feeding the toddlers soy nuggets and peas, peeling the back off cartoon plasters, throwing the babies up into the air as the sunlight dazzles them all.

Talia's brain vibrates. She almost thinks *is this real?* But knows without a doubt that it is. She feels a desperate hope, and heartbreak at the same time. What happened to her life? What happened to her children?

And then a fog descends, a noxious electrosmog that shrouds skyscrapers and blinds cars. It crashes taxis and knocks Volanters out of the sky.

People are coughing and choking, Talia's eyes are streaming. The panic is palpable: The fear is as real as the smoky air that surrounds them, leaking into ears and noses and mouths, poisoning everything in its path. It makes people act out of character. The anonymity it affords allows for small acts of violence. Talia sees someone shove a child out the way, and watches as someone else yells and punches a slow-moving woman in the face.

"Hey!" Talia yells at the attacker as the woman holds on to her cheekbone, her hands coming away with a streak of bright red. "Hey!" but no one can hear her. The panic is deafening, and she has her breathing mask on.

She's at hospital. The Gordhan. The electrosmog has caused a catastrophic Hyperloop accident. *One thousand fatalities,* her watch tells her, *and counting.*

Her heart feels as if it's beating outside her chest. The hospital corridors are a cacophony of coughing and crying, and patients bleed and moan. Nurses do their best to attend to injuries but the emergency doors keep banging open, bringing in more and more desperate people. Talia pushes her way through the crowded passages, shouting her children's names. Her voice is hoarse and tastes like ash.

By the time they had the twins' funeral a few days later, the fog had lifted, and the sky taunted her with its cheerful blue.

Rex, ashen, in a dark suit.

Talia collapsing at the water cremation.

Groundhog days of grief that felt they'd never end, hearts that were so badly broken they had parts missing and were impossible to repair. Days and days of devastation.

Talia stands up, unsteady on her feet. Now when she looks at her apartment she sees invisible evidence of the children everywhere. That's where Brett broke a window with his spinning ball, that's where Wendy vomited into the pot plant after eating too many spice cookies. But she sees something else, too. A painting hanging on the wall that she knows is not just a painting. She grabs the frame and lifts it off the wall, revealing a biometric combo-lock safe. She presses the pad of her thumb against the scanner and one of the lights turn green. The numbers come into her head without her having to think about them. She punches in 2040. The year the babies were born. The second green light glows and the lock clicks open.

Inside the safe are Wendy and Brett's birth certificates. Had they survived, they'd be celebrating their fourteenth birthdays this month. Talia clutches the laminates to her chest and sobs.

They were real.

They were real they were real they were real.

How could she have elected to forget such precious moments? To strip her life of meaning? She stands there and sways and weeps until there are no more tears left.

Talia puts the documents back and takes out the pistol. She detaches the magazine and finds it fully loaded, then clicks it back into place. Then she checks that the safety switch is on and sits down at the kitchen table, gazing at it, as she thinks about what to do next.

SEVEN
THE FOG

TALIA ARRIVES at VRLib and feels immediately overwhelmed.

The thorium-fuelled solarscraping building is gargantuan and has thirty floors of data. It's like being in a physical version of the quantum internet, but better, because it's pure truth. No GIFS of guinea pig olympics here, no memes of kittens on typewriters. Just facts and news and photographs that have been corroborated by multiple reliable sources and are beyond reproach. It's the go-to place for journalists looking to triangulate facts in a world where visual special effects have become so advanced with their match moving and digital compositing that you can't tell a fake person from the real thing.

The Virtual Reality Library was commissioned in 2034 after a cyberprankster used his home SFX software to splice up a fake clip of a famous actress being beheaded in Belarus. He hacked a major newstream's channel to flight the video and it zoomed around the globe with more than twenty-three million views before it was outed as quack. There was such an outrage that the government was forced to create a centre where only true data would exist. It became increasingly valuable every time a major news event hit the headlines and people scrambled to find out if it was true.

And invaluable to someone like me, thinks Talia, *someone who can't even trust their own memories.*

Talia goes to one of the communal desks and puts on a head-set. She dictates into the mic—*Hyperloop accident 2052*—and uses her shaking hands to scroll past the boxes and boxes of information that come up, confirming the tragedy. Her skeleton aches with sadness.

So it did happen.

Talia takes off the head-set and cradles it, then she pinches the bridge of her nose. No wonder she wanted the memories erased; they were just too painful to hold on to. She wants to cry again but keeps her nerve and blinks away the tears that are stinging her scratchy eyes. She puts the set back on.

"Fatalities," she adds, to narrow the results.

A list of names and dynap codes spool before her. There are 1,064 entries. More people died that day, the computer hastens to add. That week had an unprecedented number of deaths and injuries due to The Fog. Asthma, emphysema, acute bronchiolitis, pedestrians knocked over by Cabbies, Volanters crashing, ambudrones unable to land. The list goes on and on. Talia shivers, and forces herself to focus. A part of her is resisting hard: She doesn't want to find her kids' names on the list. She's afraid of looking and irrationally thinks of praying to someone to safeguard her beautiful children in this minute, this all-important minute. But who will she pray to? She had forsaken her god the same day he had forsaken her.

Talia takes a deep breath and starts scrolling down the list.

All these dead people, she thinks. *All with mothers and fathers and lovers.*

It's too long.

"Search this list." A search bar pops up and Talia cracks her knuckles, counts to ten. "Brett Maddox."

Five possible matches jump out in yellow and Talia's heart leaps into her throat. She blinks hard and checks the names. No Brett Maddox.

"New search," she says. "Wendy Maddox."

This time there are six possible matches, and Talia holds her breath while she checks them once, twice, three times. No Wendy Maddox. She searches again, this time using their dynap codes, and still they evade death. Talia spends the next hour checking everything she can think of: the Gordhan hospital patient roll, the city morgue's register. Not only for that day, but for the entire year, then decade. She searches the rest of the country, too, not just Johannesburg, and comes up blissfully empty-handed. Birth certificates, yes. Death certificates, no.

What had Yorke said? That you should never trust a memory.

She's so relieved she feels like melting through the floor.

Her kids are alive. Her kids are alive!

But the relief swirls with dread and anger. Where are they, what has been done to them? Her pistol thrums against her thigh.

EIGHT
DAMAGE CONTROL

YORKE ISN'T EXPECTING Talia back so soon, and he certainly isn't expecting the gun she shoves into his balls. She's got him nailed to the entrance hall wall. He's wearing a long charcoal-coloured trench coat.

"What the—"

His eyes are sparking with fright.

"You motherfucker," Talia says, pushing the barrel of the pistol harder into his crotch. "I want to know what happened."

"You know what happened," says Yorke. "I unscrambled your memory."

"I want to know *what really happened*," says Talia. "Where are my children?"

Yorke makes a pained face. "The accident."

"Bullshit!" she shouts. "They're still alive. I'm going to find them and you're going to help me."

"You're crazy," he says.

"I'll tell you what. I'm definitely crazy enough to pull this trigger."

She applies more pressure and he winces and puts up his hands. "Okay."

"You're going to tell me what happened. And if I find out that you're mindfucking me again I'll come back here and shoot you right here. You got it?"

Yorke nods.

"Say it!"

"Yes," says Yorke.

"You won't mindfuck me."

"I won't mindfuck you."

"You'll tell me everything you know."

"I'll tell you everything I know."

It occurs to Talia that Yorke is much stronger than her. He could wrestle with her, take her gun, but he doesn't. She loosens her grip, backs away, but still keeps the weapon aimed at him.

"Start from the beginning," she says.

Yorke rubs his face. "Not here. We don't have time."

"What are you talking about?"

"They'll know something's up. Because you came back here. They'll know they'll have to do damage control."

"What? Who?"

"The same people who gave me the instructions to implant the fake memory of the hospital. And the funeral."

"My children are safe?" she asks, hope like a hot stone in her throat. She didn't find evidence of their deaths, but it doesn't automatically follow that they're safe.

"Not safe," says Yorke.

Talia's stomach burns; saliva pools in her mouth. She feels like vomiting. "But they're alive?"

He looks at her and in that moment his face looks as haunted and hopeful as she feels.

"They're alive," he says.

NINE
A MATTER OF TIME

THERE'S an ear-splitting bang as a bullet ricochets off the outside of the front door, and Talia gets such a fright she almost drops her gun.

"Fuck!" Yorke grabs her hand. "They're here."

More gunshots, more pockmarks in the bullet-proof metal, and Yorke pulls Talia away from the blasts and down a dark passageway. Talia expects him to lead her out a back door, but she's sure the attackers will be there, too. He shunts her into a room—no, it's a garage—and zips a cover off a matte black sports car with a rubber-ribbed roof.

Talia knows the model. It made the news when the government had bought a fleet of them for their top officials. Kevlar coating, multi-pocket run-flat tyres, unbreakable superglass windows. They jump in, and Yorke zips her belt on. The compact car roars to life, and he jams his foot down onto the accelerator, smashing though the garage door and flying down the street. Three people in dark uniforms yell and shoot in their direction, exploding neighbours' house windows and cheap ornamental statues.

The shiny black SUV squeals into action, ready for the

chase. The uniforms jump in the side doors and they slam shut. Yorke puts his foot down.

"Who are they?" Talia's voice is hoarse with nerves.

"Agents," says Yorke, concentrating on the road.

How did they know she went back to Yorke? Were they following her? Is she carrying some kind of tracking pixel? She looks down at her wrist and sees her reflection in the cracked screen of her watch. She wrenches it off and throws it out the car.

The Cabbies zooming around them slow down and pull to the side of the road when their sensors pick up Yorke's erratic driving. Human drivers are not as smart. They swear at him and accelerate aggressively, and Talia covers her eyes as Yorke almost flattens a tuk-tuk that refuses to get out of his way. The SUV is right behind them now, and bullets fly past them. Talia feels for her pistol, wonders if she should try to return fire. Yorke puts his hand on her thigh.

"It's too dangerous," he says, then pulls his hand back to the steering wheel to dodge a motorbike. Missiles continue to ricochet off the car. Then a man with an automatic shotgun hangs out the SUV window and takes aim.

"Watch out!" she shouts, and they both duck. Five, six, seven explosions in a row and their back window finally shatters and bullets rip through the cabin. Talia quickly searches for injuries, looks for blood, but she can't see any. A slug is embedded in the back of Yorke's headrest.

Suddenly he swings the car a hard left into a small alleyway that looks way too narrow to fit a car.

"Shit!" Talia holds her breath.

Sparks fly off the sides of the car as they skim the brick walls on either side of them. Talia turns to look at the SUV. It's too wide for the lane, and it squeals and smokes as it gets stuck at the entrance.

"They're stuck!"

If Yorke is pleased, he doesn't show it. "It's just a matter of time before they find us again."

"What do they want?"

Yorke looks pointedly to the blown up back window and the ripped upholstery. "Isn't it obvious?"

He's still driving fast. Too fast.

"Where are we going?"

Yorke scrubs his hair with his knuckles. "I don't know."

They drive for ten minutes, looking for somewhere to hide the car. When Yorke sees an abandoned strip mall he yanks the wheel and smashes through the boarded-up entrance. The car, despite its modest size, is as strong as a tank. The tyres crunch over broken glass and furniture, and they roll in and park the car in one of the deserted shops. Yorke climbs out of the car to pull down the shop's rusted metal shutter.

"Milk&Silk," says Talia, when he climbs back in.

"What?"

Talia gestures at the naked, scuffed mannequinbots that lie on the broken floor tiles.

"This used to be a lingerie store. I'm surprised the Skinbots are still here," she says. "Thought they would have been looted."

"Nah," says Yorke. "Too creepy."

The inside of the car is suddenly so quiet. They look at each other, grateful to be alive.

TEN

BRITTLE PANDORA'S BOX

"I WANT TO REMEMBER WHAT HAPPENED," says Talia. "To my children."

"It's not important."

"Fuck you."

They both stare out at the trashed interior of the store. She's still shaking.

"The past won't help us now," says Yorke. "We need to be right here if we want to survive."

"I need to know what happened."

"We don't have time."

"How will I be able to find them if I can't remember—"

Yorke hits the steering wheel. Talia doesn't care that he's getting frustrated with her. All she cares about is finding her family.

"How can I find it? The memory?" she asks.

"You already have it."

"I don't! Don't you think I'd know if I did?"

"Look," says Yorke. "The agents instructed me to plant those false memories to make you think that your kids were dead, but—"

"But?"

"But that's not all I did. I don't like taking directions from anyone. And you seemed really ... smart. I kind of hoped you'd see through the fake memories. So I unscrambled your memory of what really happened, in case you were able to do that, to remember that day. You know, when they were abducted."

"So they *were* taken."

"Yes."

"But then if you've already given me back that day, why don't I remember it?"

Yorke shrugs. "It's not as simple as that. The brain's an extremely complicated organ. Maybe you're too traumatised to see it. Maybe you're not ready. Maybe you're protecting yourself from emotional pain."

"My mind is ... repressing it?"

"Exactly."

"So how do I stop it from doing that?"

Yorke laughs. "It's not like a switch you can flip."

"What if it were? A switch? How would I flip it?"

He turns to her, shakes his head. "You'd need some kind of trigger. Some kind of prompt or provocation to stimulate your memory bank."

"Like what?"

"Impossible to know. A picture, or piece of clothing. A particular scent."

"Like a sniffer dog, really," says Talia, and Yorke laughs and rubs the stubble on his chin.

"I guess so, yes."

"I don't have anything like that. I didn't even know they were alive till an hour ago."

Yorke sighs and sits back into the carseat. "It was autumn, 2048."

"What are you talking about?"

"You got there late. Half an hour late."

"Where?"

"I backed up the memory you elected to erase," says Yorke. "That day you wanted to forget."

"You viewed it? Is that even possible?"

"Talia," he says. "You're going to have to trust me."

"I do trust you," she says, surprising herself.

"Close your eyes."

She sits back and forces her eyelids down.

"Think of the day you went to collect Wendy and Brett from the Atrium."

The Atrium.

Talia's mind is blank. All she can think of is Yorke sitting next to her, the warmth coming off his strong, solid body.

"You ran inside. The Games were over."

"The Games?"

"It's an annual government-run competitive event to single out kids with special talent. Virtual reality IQ games and simulations. Japanese puzzles, archery, laser tag, that kind of thing. Kids showing promise are offered bursaries and early internships."

You viewed my memories? thinks Talia. *Viewed them often enough to know my kids' names.*

Shut up, she tells herself. *Shut up and try to remember.*

"The Games were over, and all the kids were gone. You started panicking, phoning the other parents. No one had seen the twins leave."

"I was late," she says.

"Yes."

Something is starting to stream through now, like ribbons of coloured smoke. She sees the Atrium, sees the laser tag hall. Balloons float half-heartedly in the empty, echoey space. Confetti on the floor.

Wendy! She had called. *Brett!*

She had called them over and over but she could feel that they were gone. The parents she phoned all sounded shocked and asked if they could help. Rex wasn't answering his phone.

It's as if they vanished into thin air; like that noxious fog had taken them after all. Talia held onto hope: *They had quickly run somewhere to get a snack, or they had gone home with another child, a parent Talia didn't know. They had made their own way home when she had been late; Rex had picked them up and taken them for a frozen soyshake.* But with every hour that passed, the hope faded, like a flower dying right in front of her eyes.

The policetrons arrived and checked the security cameras. Rex finally arrived, his face a white stone. He had tried to hold her, but her hands pushed him away.

Then came the screams and the stars, and the fading to black.

"Talia!"

Talia opens her eyes and sees she's in Yorke's car. His hands are on her shoulders, as if he's been shaking her.

"Talia, are you okay?"

Something has broken inside her. A brittle Pandora's box that is leaking pain like black blood, poisoning the rest of her body.

She starts crying. Loud, noisy, messy sobs that take up all the space in the cabin. Yorke holds her, tentatively at first, just an arm over her shoulders, then as she creeps into him, crawls into the alcove of his strong chest, he holds her tighter, clasping, cradling, enfolding her shattered and vulnerable body. She kisses him, and he hesitates, holds back, perhaps not wanting to take advantage of her. But she needs him, and she's ready to take what she needs.

Yorke returns her kiss, and with her sitting on his lap so ensconced by him she feels protected: Talia realises she hasn't felt safe for a long, long time.

Their kisses get deeper, more urgent, and Talia zips off her jumpsuit, stopping only to unclip her gun from her thigh and toss it on the dashboard. She lifts Yorke's T-shirt and is surprised again by his muscles, his tattoos, his scars. He opens the car door and carries her to a corner where discarded shop linen lies like a nest on the floor, then takes off his pants. His face is nothing but desire. His voice is gruff.

"Are you sure?"

"It's the only thing I'm sure of," Talia says.

Talia's only craving in this moment is to be utterly consumed by Yorke. She wants him all over her, and inside her. She wants to be filled up by him. She kisses him hard, runs her hands over his shoulders, his chest. For a split second she feels like they have known each other forever and this makes her feel safer still, and increases her craving for his touch. Her whole body is pulsing with desire, like flashing red light. She needs him inside her right now.

"I need to tell you something," Yorke says.

"Not now."

She reaches for him, and he enters her, pushing pleasure into every nerve in her body. She gasps with the unexpected joy of it, her body arches, and Yorke kisses her face and neck and starts his slow, swollen, thrusting.

They both know they're risking their lives.

Talia, eyes closed, imagines it's Rex that's inside her, and she's overcome with the emotion and thrill of it, and she feels her pleasure rolling beside her, inside her, till she can't breathe anymore.

Rex, she thinks, *my Rex. You've come back to me.*

Yorke increases his pace and depth, and Talia sobs and groans and bites his shoulder, and they fall off the cliff together.

ELEVEN

SPINNING RUBIK'S CUBE

"I KNOW someone who can help us," says Talia as she pulls on her clothes. She'd love to lie in Yorke's arms, would love to rest against his strong body.

Yorke buckles his pants, and she can't help looking at his scars. They seem so neat, so uniform. There's still so much she wants to know, but getting to safety first seems like the best course of action. No way she'll be able to find her kids while she has a team of assassins after her. Besides, if anyone can help her, with all her security contacts, Monique can.

Talia realises it makes sense now that Monique was always urging her to forget Rex. Rex was part of a painful past that Talia had, herself, elected to forget. It must have been difficult for her best friend to navigate Talia's weird half-baked reality. Talia feels a rush of tenderness for her.

"Who?" says Yorke, pressing his remote to open the car doors for them.

"An old friend. She works at KALI. If anyone can keep us safe, it's her."

Something shifts in Yorke's face. "Can you trust her?"

"Of course I can trust her. She's cool. You'll see."

Yorke gives his long charcoal trench coat to Talia.

"Put it on," he says. "It's triple kevlar with graphene lining."

"I don't know what that means."

"It means it's bullet-proof and bomb-proof."

Talia pulls it on; it's big for her, so she belts the waist. They climb in the car and Talia uses the car's phone to make the call.

"Monique," she says when her friend's face appears in the hologram.

"Jesus!" she says. "Where are you? I've been so worried."

"I'm ... I'm in an abandoned lingerie store."

"What?"

"Never mind the details. I'm in trouble. I need your help. Can we meet somewhere?"

"Of course! Will you come in? I'll let security know to expect you."

"I'm with someone."

"You're with someone? Who?"

"It's a long story."

"You have to come alone. I can't get clearance for some random you just picked up."

"He knows things ... about what happened."

"What are you talking about?"

"I'll explain when we get there."

"No. You can't bring him. I won't be able to get him in here. Let him drop you off."

"I can't. They're after him, too. They'll kill him."

"What? Who?"

"He saved my life."

Monique sighs. "Alright. Fuck. I'll make a plan."

MONIQUE'S WAITING for them when they arrive, arms folded in front of her, wearing her smart military jacket. The roboguards at the front had scanned them for their dynap codes and taken away Talia's pistol. Her thigh feels naked without it.

"This is Yorke," says Talia. They share a cursory nod, and Monique leads them inside the building. She seems cold: perhaps she's angry with Talia for bringing him along.

"I've got so much to tell you," says Talia.

Monique regards her coolly. "Let's go somewhere we can talk."

Doors slide and lock behind them as they go. They wind around the main building and head west, towards the security branch. When they reach KALI, Monique opens a huge white double-door and they follow her inside. Talia's expecting some kind of boardroom but it's a tech lab with white walls and counters and machinery that looks like it's from the future.

"What is this place?" asks Talia.

The doors click closed behind them, which makes Talia glance backwards, and her blood runs cold. Four agents, dressed head-to-toe in black, stand at attention. The same agents that had shot up Yorke's house and had tried to kill them. When Talia turns back to face Monique, her friend has a large black gun pointed at her.

The click of the safety switch being turned off is devastating.

"No," she says, and grabs her lurching stomach. *No no no, this can't be happening.*

Talia drags her eyes towards Yorke, but no shock registers on his face.

"Damn it, Talia," Monique says through clenched teeth. "When are you going to learn to just let things go?"

Talia can't talk for a moment; her shock bleaches her thoughts.

"Let things go?" she says, trying to swallow the thickness in her throat. "Forget my children?"

"We gave you every possible chance to let them go and move on with your life."

Yorke is unflustered. "The agency recruited the children and then engineered a new reality for you, one where you wouldn't miss them. Wouldn't know they had ever existed. That was the idea, anyway."

"It's impossible."

"Not really," says Monique. "It's worked in dozens of other cases. I don't know why you've been so stubborn."

"Stubborn? They're *my children*," says Talia. She wants to add: *and you should know. You were there for all of it.* But then when she searches her unscrambled memories for Monique's face she comes up empty. She wasn't at any of the birthday parties, the special outings, the family lunches.

"Oh my god," Talia says. "It was all made up. Our friendship was made up. Fake memories, like the Hyperloop accident."

"Yes," says Monique. "Although we did meet up a few times in the last year. It was our way of keeping tabs on you, making sure you didn't remember anything you shouldn't have."

"That didn't go according to plan," says Yorke.

Monique narrows her eyes at him. "Quite."

"So you two know each other," says Talia, still trying to piece it all together. Her mind is a spinning Rubik's Cube and she doesn't know which memories to trust.

"No," says Yorke. "It's the minions I know. They broke

into my house and put a gun to my head. Briefed me on the job to plant the false Hyperloop memory. Said if I didn't do it they'd kill us both. It seemed like the only solution."

Talia turns to him. "How did that business card—your business card—get into my house? Into my kitchen?"

"I put it there."

"What? How?"

"As much as I'm loving this little catch-up," says Monique, "I think it's best to get on to more serious matters." She gestures to one of the agents. "Bring them in."

The agent nods and walks to an interleading door, holds his thumb up to the biometric pad, and the door beeps and glides open.

On the other side stand Wendy and Brett. Talia feels her knees buckle.

TWELVE

SECOND SKIN

BRETT AND WENDY are both a foot taller than Talia remembers them, and they look like cyborg soldiers. Roscoe guns built into their forearms, graphene helmets, steel-plated shoulders. Their irises are glazed over with some kind of cybernetic lenses, and when they look at Talia, their eyes remain cold.

Talia yelps and runs unsteadily over to them, hugs Wendy, and then pulls Brett into the hug, too. Tears blur her vision and burn her nose. The children remain still, and silent. Their metallic parts are cold against her skin, and the chill seems to enter her body and travel deep inside, to her core.

"Wendy," Talia says, pulling away to look at her daughter's face. "What have they done to you?"

They are both so calm, so composed, but Talia feels like there's a hurricane in her heart.

"Brett?" she says, wiping her tears on her sleeve. Her son looks at her and blinks. His exosuit ripples with baked-in invisitech camouflage, giving the appearance of his body disappearing against the background. They both ripple like those deep-sea fish who pulse with colour according to their environment.

"What have you done to them?" Talia whirls around and shouts at Monique. "What have you done to them?"

The agents take a step forward.

"Aren't they magnificent?" says Monique.

"They're ... weapons," says Talia.

"They're the new age of soldiers. Their modifications are on the cutting edge of military tech. Every element has been designed, implemented and tested to uphold our highest standards. Brett and Wendy are our most successful transformations. So much so, that our operation—which used to be a top secret experiment—will now be rolled out in earnest. It's going to change everything. South Africa will be at the forefront of militech—"

"They're fourteen years old," says Yorke.

"Yes," says Monique. "Their alterations will expand with them as they grow. Their age is the best time to reconstruct. They grow into their advancements and it becomes like a second skin."

"They're fourteen years old," says Yorke again.

Talia feels vomit climb up her throat.

"Don't you see that we're saving the world?" says Monique. "The Northern Hemisphere arms race. The water wars. The threat of extra-terrestrials. It's not a matter of if we'll need them. It's a matter of when. South Africa will be the safest and most protected country in the world."

"At what cost?" says Yorke.

"The plan, now that we're rolling it out, is to only take two children in every thousand."

Talia's head is buzzing. "What?"

"Sacrifices have to be made for the good of the country."

Talia stares at the faces she used to know so well.

"So you decided to sacrifice my children."

"It's not personal."

"It's barbaric," says Yorke.

"Point two per cent of the teen population is nothing compared to the antiquated conscription model. *That* was barbaric. In those days you sent your kid to war and you didn't expect him to come back. These young soldiers, on the other hand, are primed for war. They've got every possible advantage. Camo-kevlarskin, Graphene skull-nets, radial roscoes with heat-seeking bullets. They'll fight, and they'll win."

"Why them?" asks Talia. "That day at the Atrium. Why did you choose them?"

"They were the strongest, healthiest, brightest kids. Their MediSlate Verve level was higher than anyone else in the class. Plus, they volunteered," says Monique.

"Bullshit."

"They won that laser tag competition at The Games by a country mile. They have innate talent: great aim, staying power, and killer instinct. Their points that day were in the top one percentile of the whole class. When I handed them their prizes, I asked them if they'd ever consider fighting for their country. They both said yes."

"They were twelve!" says Talia.

"Truly selfless. Perfect for the job."

The children stand in silence, blinking.

"So you kidnap the kids that show promise, and brain-bleach the parents. Plant false memories of accidents and funerals."

"It seems less traumatic that way."

"What about Rex?" Talia asks. "Did you brainbleach him, too?"

"Rex disappeared after we recruited Wendy and Brett."

"You didn't take him?"

"No."

So he did leave her. Left her when she needed him the most.

"And those social media pictures of him sailing around the world with that woman?" Talia says.

"Computer generated. Quite obviously so, in my opinion, although we did have our best team on it. You were just too blinded by grief to notice anything amiss. It was supposed to encourage you to move on."

The social media pictures were fake.

Rex needed to disappear before they brain bleached him, too.

And he needed to come back as a different person.

Yorke's business card was in her kitchen.

The truth starts to roll towards Talia, soft and slow, and then it gains momentum and threatens to knock her over. She turns to Yorke and her jaw hangs open, her chest swells.

"Rex," she says, breathless.

The cosmetic surgery, the contact lenses, the tattoos. Perfect teeth that must be caps. That blue-black hair that seems so obviously dyed, now.

"Rex," she says again, trying to breathe, trying to not fall over with the realisation that Rex is right here with her, that he'd never really left her.

The business card in her apartment could only have been left by Rex. He still had his keys. She should have known ... but her head has been such a mess since this all started ... but she should have known that feeling she has when she's with him.

It's Rex.

She launches into his arms. Despite where they are and

what has happened, she throws herself into him and he holds her, squeezes the air out of her.

"God I've missed you," he whispers into her hair, rubs his lips on her cheeks. "Having you so close. It's been torture."

Talia feels her tears begin to sting again but she fights them. There's no time to cry.

"But you knew about this. This place. Monique."

"I've been investigating since the kids were taken. I didn't know the extent of it."

"But you knew. You knew we were coming in to see Monique. Why did you let me come here?"

"It was the only way I could get in. And I needed to get in to be able to save the kids."

"Sorry to break up the sweetheart reunion," says Monique, "but we need to go."

Two of the agents fall into place to guard Monique, and the other two stay behind.

Talia spins around. "Go where?"

"I'm going upstairs to file a report. You're going to go with Wendy and Brett."

"You're going to wipe our memories again," says Talia.

Monique pauses. "Let's go with that."

"They can't wipe it again," says Rex. "Not without doing real damage."

"Why would they care?"

"You'll be more of a problem. Better to erase you—us —altogether."

"You wouldn't," says Talia. "Monique. You wouldn't."

"I'm not going to be the one pulling the trigger," she says, gesturing at the children. "Wendy, Brett, you have your orders."

"Yes ma'am," they say in unison, and raise their roscoes,

snick the switches. Long, smooth, steel barrels raise out of their forearms. Their index fingers have been modified: transformed into triggers.

"Please, follow us," says Wendy, as if she's about to take them to another room, for tea, instead of putting a bullet in their brains.

Rex holds her hand and whispers to her. "Stay close," he says.

THIRTEEN

A SOFT SCUFFLE

"ARE YOU READY?" says Brett. "It's time to go."

Monique leaves the room, and the two remaining agents motion for Talia and Rex to follow the children. They stand there, in a huddle, Talia not wanting to leave. She reaches out and touches Wendy: puts her palm on her pale cheek, moves it down to her shoulder.

"My beautiful girl," she says. "You were always so clever, and warm, and funny." Then she turns to Brett. "Brett. You were the serious one, but so generous and empathic."

The female agent is getting impatient. "Come on," she says. "Let's move it." But Talia ignores her and steps closer to Wendy.

"Do you remember," says Talia, swallowing the huge lump in her throat. "Do you remember that day ... that day we visited the sculpture gardens. We ate iced coconuts. Dad carried you on his shoulders, Wendy, remember? Brett held my hand. We took off our shoes and danced to the music, right there on the lawns, not caring what anyone thought of us."

Rex clears his throat. Talia can see tears in his eyes, too.

"Do you remember that? Brett?"

Brett's face doesn't change.

"Wendy?" says Talia. "Do you remember?"

Wendy blinks her cold eyes. There's nothing there, no spark of recognition, no warmth.

Talia runs her hand down Wendy's arm, as if to hold her hand, but then grabs her roscoe arm and pulls her trigger finger, firing a shot into Brett's neck. He gasps in shock, and his hands travel up to the wound, which is pulsing with bright red blood. Talia swings the gun towards the agents and shoots them, too, in the forehead, and they fall to the floor. Then she turns the gun on Wendy, shoves it right into her jugular, and pulls the trigger. She feels the projectile enter the girl's head and tangle her brains as the skull-net keeps the bullet in, and then Wendy collapses, and Talia looks at Rex's shocked face.

"Run!"

Rex is rooted to the floor with shock. He can't tear himself away from the bodies of the children.

"We have to run," says Talia. "Now!"

She picks up the agents' weapons from their unlaced hands, one for each of them, and Rex tears the silver chain with a dog-tag access chip from the corpse's neck.

"How did you know?" Rex says.

"Wendy has a small birthmark under her ear. Brett has a scar under his eyebrow. Those things," she looks at the cyborgs, "have neither."

She passes him a gun, and they run through the open door, into a passage. Rex uses the dog-tag to open the next door, and the room is empty. He opens another lab, a board-room, a hall. They hear running above them, and weapons being loaded.

"Hurry," says Talia.

The next room has people in it. Talia jumps back from the doorway when she sees them, as if she's had an electric shock. There are rows and rows of cyborgs with their guns pointed at Talia and Rex. A sea of Wendys and Bretts. Talia and Rex bolt, but the soldiers follow them like high-tech zombies. There's a gunshot, and another, and soon there are bullets zinging all over the corridor. Talia and Rex shoot as many soldiers as they can, but their bullets ricochet off the bulletproof suits. Talia shoots one of the Bretts in the neck, Rex gets one in the forehead, but more and more come. There must be fifty of the killing machines.

There's a loud bang and Talia falls down. There's a roaring pain in her calf. She calls out loudly as she hits the ground.

No, she thinks, *no. I'm not going to die like this.*

The clones are ready to swarm over them, and Rex keeps shooting and wrenches Talia up from the ground. Her weight slows him down.

"Leave me!" she says, but Rex's face is set and he lifts her higher off the ground and speeds up.

"Leave me, or we'll both be killed."

Never, his body is saying. *Never.*

There's one more door to try, and Rex opens it and they fall inside the dark space. They shoot five cyborgs that try to enter behind them, then the door closes, and they are safe, if only for a moment.

In the dark Talia rolls on the floor and grabs her calf where she's been shot. She can feel the hot blood coursing down her leg and the bullet burns her as if it is alight.

Rex reaches out for her, breathing hard. "Are you okay?"

She's about to answer when she hears a shuffling sound behind her. A soft scuffle. There are other people in this room.

FOURTEEN
BLOOD FRECKLES

"MOM?" says a thin voice. The light comes on. "Dad?"

Talia wheels around, forgetting the pain in her leg. In that moment she sees nothing but the haunted, happy faces of her children. She cries out and the kids tumble into them, and her heart balloons as she feels the reassuring weight of them on her, touches their limbs, presses into them and feels bones and flesh and warm skin. They're wearing thin hospital gowns. She searches them for signs of abuse, of alteration, but there is none. No blades or guns, just a train track of blood freckles on the tender parts of their arms where they've had their red cells harvested over and over.

"You're bleeding," says Brett.

"Don't worry about me," says Talia. She has so much to say to them, wants to keep them in her arms, but the noise outside is getting louder. The cyborgs will bash or shoot their way in soon and there's no time for anything except to find a way out.

Talia drags herself to the opposite wall, the boundary she knows is the one keeping them from the outside world. There must be a way to break it down.

Rex takes her arm. "Talia," he says.

"We need to find a way out," she says. There is a gunshot at the door, then another. They are shooting out the lock.

"There are no other doors," says Wendy. "That's the only one."

Another bullet punctures the door just above the handle.

"Talia," says Rex again, guiding her face to look at him. "Monique and the agents will be here in a minute. They'll open the door and we'll all be killed."

"No!" shouts Talia. She gathers the weapons of the dead clones and hands them out to her kids.

"It won't be enough," he says, softly. "Four of us, versus ... all of them."

Talia knows it's true.

There is a hush outside, and the shooting stops. Monique arrives behind the door. "Talia," she says. "Rex. I need you to listen."

"Fuck you," yells Talia, and checks her weapon. She's desperate to get a bullet into Monique's brain.

"She wants the kids," says Rex. "She needs them alive."

"I'm going to open the door," says Monique.

"If you open that door my face is the last thing you'll ever see!" shouts Talia.

"Okay, okay," says Monique. "Keep calm. I'm here to negotiate."

"It's a bit late for that."

"Send the kids out," says Monique. "At least make sure they're safe."

Talia splutters. "*Safe,* with you?"

"I have fifty soldiers here with a hundred bullets a piece. There's not going to be much left of this room when they're finished with it. Now, I'm giving you a chance to save your children. Send them out, and they won't be harmed."

"No way," says Wendy, shaking her head. "No way."

"We're staying with you," says Brett. "Even if it means dying."

Rex grips Talia's arm. "That won't be necessary. I need you all to listen to me very carefully."

FIFTEEN
SMOKE AND SIRENS

"TALIA, you and the kids are going to crouch down into that corner there."

Rex points to the corner of the room. It's the furthest from the wall that stands between them and freedom.

"You're going to cover yourselves with the kevlar coat. All over. Make sure everything is covered. Do you understand?"

The shooting has started again, and the door lock rings as it's hit. There is pushing from the other side. They have a few seconds left.

"What about you?" says Talia. Rex doesn't have a shred of protective clothing.

"I'm going to do what I have to, to protect you and the children."

Talia's mind whirrs. *What?*

"As soon as they break through that door I'm going to blow up the room. Kill them all. It's the only way to ensure your safety."

Talia stares at him, she can't talk.

"If I don't stop them now, they'll never leave you alone. They'll hunt you down."

"How are you going to—?"

Before Talia finishes her question, she understands the answer. She looks at Rex's neat surgical scars and realises what they are. She remembers his house, remembers the bomb equipment on the shelf. Sheet explosive.

"Memories aren't the only things you can implant," he says.

"No!" she cries. "No!" and the kids are around them, asking what is happening. She grabs Brett's head and holds it to her burning, aching chest. Rex gives Wendy a huge bear hug, and then they all hug each other.

Rex kisses Talia on the mouth, and his eyes are electric.

"I love you," he says. "Never stopped loving you."

The chasmic love and grief Talia feels makes her want to melt into the floor. How can she lose Rex again? Part of her wants to hold his hand while he detonates the bombs and die right there with him in a blaze of light, but then she looks at Wendy and Brett and knows she has to live.

The door flies open and there's a blur of Monique and her agents, and the rippling, camo-suited army of cyborgs.

"Now!" says Rex, and Talia grabs the kids and pushes them into the corner. Rex watches them to make sure they're safely covered by the coat, then touches the screen on his watch. There are three quick beeps, and there is an explosion so loud Talia is sure she'll be permanently deafened by it. Scalding heat, even through the coat, as she holds on to her children. Things hit them: bullets, shrapnel, detritus, blown-up bodies, while Wendy screams and Brett breathes hard.

Talia waits for silence, then lowers the protective material. Bodies everywhere. Blood.

Smoke and sirens.

Cool air blows in from outside where she can see trees, and the overcast sky. The wall and half the ceiling lie smashed on the floor. Talia feels cold, so very cold. She thinks of the ice floe and glowing icebergs in Antarctica. She thinks of the cold black pool in her dreams.

She pulls the children up and they make their way outside, picking over severed limbs and burning bricks. Wendy's hair is grey with dust, and Brett's ears are bleeding. They all weep as they climb over the rubble, breathing in the acrid fumes of the blast.

Talia limps; her leg is throbbing, but not as much as her heart, which is aching as if she's lying at the bottom of that dark pool. She urges herself to be strong. They are so close to freedom, and she has her children to look after.

Brett pauses, bends to look at something, and Talia pulls him sharply.

"Don't look," she says, wiping her tears.

Some things you can never erase from your memory.

They step out into the cool, grey air. There would be no more looking back.

ABOUT JT LAWRENCE

JT Lawrence is an Amazon bestselling author and playwright. She lives in Parkview, Johannesburg, in a house with a red front door.

If you enjoyed 'The Memory Hacker'
you'll love JT Lawrence's futuristic thriller series
'When Tomorrow Calls'.

Be notified of giveaways & new releases by signing up to JT's mailing list via Facebook or at

www.jt-lawrence.com

facebook.com/JanitaTLawrence

twitter.com/pulpbooks

amazon.com/author/jtlawrence

bookbub.com/profile/jt-lawrence

MELTING SHLEMIEL

JASON WERBELOFF

WHAT WOULD YOU SACRIFICE TO
BE FREE?

Shlemiel discovers a way to melt his impenetrable skin, but
at a terrible cost.

How will he choose between sacrificing his happiness and
the safety of those he loves?

ONE

SHOTGUNS FOR SHABBOS

THE OLD WOMAN reached over the counter, and punched me in the jaw. "Three microwave emitters," her quaking knuckles vibrated.

I tried to hide my smile. The older generation preferred fist-to-face communication, as it had been in the old days before the advent of thrumming tech.

My overlay automatically noted the order.

3x MICROWAVE UNITS

The translucent text appeared across my vision. I was about to message her the invoice, when I realized she probably didn't have a working overlay to read it. I beat her over the crown of her head instead, thrumming out the price with my knuckles. "That will be sixty shekels, Mrs. Katz."

She paused, and I thought I'd have to beat her again, harder this time. But then she nodded. Reached into her purse, and produced an ancient credit card. Here at Mendel's Butchery, we kept the only working card machine this side of King George Street. Stroke of genius on Mendel's behalf, if you asked me. All the old rollers came here because of it. They shuffled in, falling over themselves, waving their credit cards. I had to pick them up. Them, and their credit cards. That was half my job. When I wasn't falling over myself.

My real name, the name Mother had written on my birth certificate, is Shlomo. That had changed when my parents found I couldn't walk ten paces without breaking something. That was before my bar mitzvah. Before I was shelled.

"Oy vey," Father would say. "Not the Ming." Or, "Oy, not the 3D printer."

Mother would sigh. Ruffle my hair with her tremendous stony mitts. "My Shlemiel."

The name had stuck.

I was about to take the old woman's card from her when she withdrew it. "Shlemiel," she said through a weak fist to my temple, "my son tells me you have fresh cathode ray tubes. Delicious radiation levels."

Lazy to reach over the counter again and whack the old woman over the head, I nodded instead, pointing to a sign perched on the counter.

MATURED CATHODE RAY TUBES
75 SHEKELS

From between her hunched shoulders, Mrs. Katz screwed up her leathery eyes. Craned her neck. Stared at the credit card for a long moment. Then back to the sign.

She socked me in the nose. "Just the microwave emitters, please."

I nodded. Accepted her credit card.

While I put through the payment on the antiquated machine, ridiculous with its pin codes rather than biometrics, I scratched the bridge of my nose. My carapaced fingers felt the contours of my nostrils. Or, at least, where my nostrils had once been.

The old woman brought me back to awareness with an uppercut to the chin. "You get used to it," her knuckles said.

I knew I would. Eventually. It had been five years since my bar mitzvah. Five years since I was shelled. To think, before the ceremony there'd been nothing I'd wanted more than to look like my parents. To tread with Father's footsteps, heavy enough to chip the marble floor. To crack walnuts with a flick of the wrist, like Mother did. But I had been Shlemiel, the only child, who'd break his arm one week and the patio table the next.

"Check twice before you cross, Shlemiel," Mother would call out.

"Make sure you use oven gloves before you open the stove, Shlemiel."

"Take a sweater with you, Shlemiel."

To my parents' considerable relief, the day came around shortly after my thirteenth birthday when they could finally protect me. Place me in my second skin. My shell.

It didn't help protect the patio furniture, but it did prevent more broken bones. Once the carapace had set a few hours later around my fleshy body, I was impervious to harm, and Mama's ubiquitous cautions had ceased.

In their place, Mama had developed a serenity I hadn't noticed in her before my bar mitzvah. Even through the carapace over her face – I had only ever seen her with her shell – I noticed her features relax over the months that followed. I'd imagined her fleshy cheeks, her thin lips, beneath the shell softening a little more each day.

Not only did she no longer have to worry about my safety, she didn't have to cook organic food just for me anymore. Now that I'd grown up, now that I had a shell, I had no mouth to ingest food. The exoskeleton covered all my orifices. Which meant I could eat with my parents. Eat what all the adults in Jerusalem ate.

Energy.

"See you next week," Mrs. Katz rapped on my shoulder.

I slapped her across the cheek, "Thank you for coming to Mendel's Butchery."

Her wrinkled carapace screwed up in smile, and she hobbled out the store.

I glanced up at the LED clock hanging on the tiled wall. 16:14

Shabbos would come in at around half past five. Time to go.

I neatened my desk. Stuck my foot through the back door. "Done for today," I called out. My shell translated my speech into a series of vibrations, which thrummed through my foot, into the tiled floor. A moment later, a new, fainter set of vibrations tingled my toes – Old Man Mendel's reply. "Have a good Shabbos."

I gave the Butchery a once over. All my tools were packed away. Angle grinder. Tweezers. Circular saws. Screwdrivers. Everything in their place.

I tapped the screen on the front door to read CLOSED, and opened the latch. A thousand thoughts buzzed through my carapaced head as I stepped into the Jerusalem afternoon.

Mother needed help with the waste bucket before Shabbos came in. I'd promised I'd take it out last night, but if I hurried home I might catch the waste disposal truck as it drove past on its last round before Shabbos.

She'd want help with dinner too. Lighting the twin

nuclear reactors before sunset. Preparing the firearms for the evening meal. Mother had brought home birdshot especially for tonight's guests, the Goldsteins from three streets down. Mother had a quiet feud running against Mrs. Goldstein, trying to top her dinner last week – an antique revolver blast point blank to the temple. Hence Mother's whipping out the shotguns for mains. Mama would want the best birdshot pellets we had, loaded and ready, and the guns oiled. Lest the barrels jam as they had last time the Goldsteins had come over. You could almost see Mama's blush through her carapace.

Plenty to do. I'd have to dress in my suit for synagogue too. Get everything done before –

The ground slipped out from beneath me, and the singed façade of a nearby building disappeared as the sky gyrated into my field of vision. I heard the ground collide with the back of my head as a soft thump through the shell.

"Dammit," I thrummed to myself.

If my nostrils and mouth weren't covered by the shell, I would have sighed.

Mendel would have something to say about this. I'd have to yell to him to help me up, unless someone walked by. They'd all be on their way to Shabbos, in a hurry to get their thousand tasks completed before the day was up.

My eyes found the shimmering meniscus of the Jerusalem Bubble above. The Bubble erected a decade before I was born – at least that's what they taught us in history class. Sometimes I wondered about those history teachers. Whether we, the Israelis, were in fact the first to use Bubble tech. Had the New Yorkers followed in our footsteps as the teachers said? Which seemed odd, since the New York Bubble was often called Bubble One.

Those high school history classes percolated through my mind. Ms. Segal telling us about how the Bubble had not been enough for many. In India they had submerged their Bubbles, fixing them to the ocean floor. And here in Jerusalem, although it provided more protection against missiles than the previous iron dome, it didn't protect against threats from within the city limits. Suicide bombers, knife-wielding terrorists. Worse – reformed Jewish sects who insisted their set of beliefs, their special brand of the religion, was correct above all others.

The Bubbles had proliferated. Forcefields within forcefields. First between communities, then within them. Families encapsulated themselves apart from other families.

Then came the shells.

Bubble tech taken to its logical conclusion. A forcefield, grown into an organic, impenetrable carapace that molded to an individual. Not separate from him. Natural. Like a second skin.

Lying on the sidewalk outside Mendel's Butchery now, I cursed my shell. It may have protected me from just about any impingement imaginable, but it was a nightmare when I fell on my back.

Which I did. Often.

Knowing it would be of no help at all, I tried to leverage myself onto my elbows, and flip onto my feet. I'd seen it done a rare handful of times. Once a shelled person fell on their back, it was almost impossible to stand up again without help.

"I heard you falling all the way from my desk," said Mendel, loping out of the shop. "Come on, let's get you up."

I took Old Man Mendel's hand, and he hoisted me. His shelled hand was hard in mine. A man who'd handled countless electronics in his time. Sifting through the detritus of pre-Bubble humanity, finding the juiciest radioactive elements and selling them on to the hungry populace.

I stood. Half thanked him, half apologized.

"Shlemiel." He grunted. "All I can say is thank God you have a shell." He glanced to the heavens, whether to look to the almighty for patience or to roll his stony eyes, I wasn't sure.

"Sorry," I thrummed quietly, and dusted myself off. Which was futile, since walking through the streets was a dusty business. Fine, white particles, which would have gotten into every orifice I had, if I'd had orifices at all. I thought back to my days as a child when I'd struggled to breathe in the smog and dust storms. Perhaps the shelling had been a good idea after all.

"Children," Old Man Mendel grunted, and waved me off.

I hurried home. A little slower now. Mendel wouldn't be so genial picking me up a second time.

Down King George. Three blocks. Right up Bnei Brit. Right into Ethiopia.

There.

The slim stone building was two stories high. A sliver of home, set between two others much the same. I'd barely walked through the entranceway when Mother called out from the kitchen. "Did you take out the waste?"

She knew I hadn't. Knew I was supposed to do it last night. But this was her way of sparing me. Treating me as an adult, is how Father described it. "Your mother and I won't always be here to take care of you," he'd said last week. He'd sat me down. Took my hand in his. "You need to learn how to care for a household of your own. So you can take a wife one day. One day soon."

I'd never seen my father quite so serious. The crevasse

in his brow. The severity of his carapaced eyes. "It's important you find someone." He'd cleared his throat. Spoke
quickly. As though what he was about to say was either
shameful, or obvious. Or both. "Someone of our faith.
Preferably of our sect."

I'd nodded. Of course I had. I had every intention of
marrying within the faith. How could he have thought
otherwise?

I walked through the front door. "Hi Ma," I thrummed,
on my way through the kitchen. I elbowed her hard in the
neck as I skipped past, a gesture of affection my mother had
insisted on since I was a child – less painful for me now that
I was shelled. Her shell vibrated with affection.

I was out the back door, sidling around the back of the
house. Found the waste tank, and decanted half of the
radioactive sludge into the municipal bucket. The tarred
substance sloshed into the container, piling atop itself in
viscus globs. This was the only chore I hated. That said, it
was a lot more sanitary than cleaning the organic waste my
fleshy body had produced before my shelling.

I glanced at the chronometer on my overlay.

17:20

Twelve minutes until Shabbos came in. I dashed to the
front of the house. Left the bucket on the edge of the street
where Hymie from the waste company would pick it up any
minute.

I was back inside. Oiling the shotguns. Loading the
birdshot. Aligning the weapons around the table, each
pointed lovingly at a chair. I hoped the Goldsteins appreci-
ated the effort Mama had gone to planning this dinner.
How she'd set up automated timers for each weapon,
ensuring they went off at just the right moment during the

meal, without anyone having to press a trigger and break the Shabbos.

This meal was going to be delicious.

My stomach rumbling, I tore up the stairs in threes, my shelled feet pounding the carpeted landings. I opened my cupboard. Removed my only set of clothes.

I watched my carapaced hands in the mirror, pulling up my pants. Buttoning my shirt. Shabbos was the only time I ever wore clothes. Once you were shelled, there was no need for clothes. The carapace was good for any weather, and it was featureless, an obsidian shell that stretched from my feet to the crown of my head. The flesh beneath could have been any shape. The shell masked it in a smooth, oval structure, with arms and legs jutting from its corners.

My suit buttoned, I was downstairs just in time to watch my mother light the nuclear reactors to bring in the Sabbath. This was not, strictly speaking, a son's duty. Over generations past, mothers and their daughters had performed the ritual back when they still used candles. But Mother said she liked having me around. Wanted me in the room as she stoked the uranium. She said it made her feel whole.

My duty done, I checked the yarmulke was firm on the crown of my shell, and went to my parents' bedroom. Father was donning his broad suit jacket. There was something mystical, something that would have smelled like old musk and mothballs, in the way the man moved. Would have smelled that way, had I nostrils to smell it. I watched instead. Listened to him through the vibrations in the carpet as he hummed a tune.

"Let's go," he said, and lambasted my shoulders.

"You're looking a little brittle," said Mother as we

stepped together, the three of us, to the front door. "Sure you don't want a shot before we go? We won't be eating for hours yet."

I shook my head. Sighed.

Mother wasn't hearing it. She fished around in a drawer, and found a .22. It was already loaded. Impatient, I waited as she pointed it at my forehead, and pulled the trigger.

"Feel better?"

I wobbled on my feet for a moment, enjoying the ripple of energy coursing through my shell. Despite my resistance to her mothering, I felt invigorated.

She planted a kiss on the spot where the shot had landed. "Come on, my Shlemiel."

⸻

THE ANCIENT BUILDING that was the synagogue was lit only by candlelight. This wasn't obligatory – it was permissible to use electrical lighting on Shabbos, provided one didn't flip a switch. But the shul, located in one of the more stringent areas of Mea Shearim, prided itself on an extreme orthodoxy. A Luddite adherence to the scriptures, which Mother and Father found charming. I didn't see the harm.

I ducked under the low-hanging doorway, into the firelit hall. Shadows and light danced across the walls, galvanized by the thrumming chatter of the congregants making their way to the service.

I was eighteen now, well past my coming of age. Nevertheless, I preferred not to join the main ceremony. I could if I wanted to, but it always seemed so ... loud. The water carried too many thoughts.

I did what I always did, slipping away to the overflow ceremony, the smaller mikvah, or pool, to the side of the main hall. The younger adult congregants tended to flock there. I preferred their energy. Fewer in number, but more excitable.

I descended the spiraled staircase, vibrating the stone beneath my shelled feet. With each step the temperature fell. Moisture dampened the oscillations of my thrummers.

Three twists of the stairwell, and I was on the dimly lit landing area leading to the mikvah. A line of booths beckoned, their open doors hungry for congregants. I was the first to arrive.

I disrobed, my featureless carapace glistening in the candlelight, and stepped into one of the furthest cubicles. I preferred to be on the edge of the pool, where I could listen to the congregants pray through the water, rather than have my own weak voice ripple through the pool.

I wondered whether Yonatan and Yael would be here tonight. More often than not, the Goldstein twins accompanied their parents to the main pool upstairs. But when they did join the overflow, their prayers filled the water with an earnest intensity that few of the other congregants could match.

They weren't here yet. Nor was anyone else.

I hung my suit on a hook on the back of the door, and shut the cubicle, banishing the last echoes of candlelight from the booth.

I stretched out a toe. Sunk my foot into the water with barely a slosh. This was my favorite part of the service. The moment when the water worked its magic.

I felt it first as a tingle in my heels. A wavelike motion on my ankles, fizzling and popping, as the shell melted in the holy water. It started at my feet, working up my goose-bumped legs. The sensation snaked around my buttocks, up my navel. Over my chest, coursing down my arms. Wrapping around my neck until –

I was naked.

Knowing I shouldn't, knowing it was improper, I ran my fingertips along my fleshy biceps. Tickled my pink forearms. At least, I imagined they were pink. Imagined them smooth and hairless. Raw and nude. I had no idea what they looked like exactly, since the cubicle was entirely dark. The only sensation I had was a newfound sense of hearing, my ears suddenly exposed to the world. My eyes, accustomed to the dark filter of my shell, would be blinded by anything brighter than shadows. My nose would overwhelm my brain with sensation if the cubicle had smelled of anything at all. It didn't.

In the dark wetness, the sloshing water curled around my ankles. Soon, the evening's prayers would begin, and I would hear them through the water. Hear them as vibrations carried through the liquid, up my legs and interpreted through the thrummers in my knees. Until then, I waited. Trying not to touch myself. Trying to focus on the prayers that would come next. To remember, without having to follow on my overlay, the series of prayers in the evening's davening.

I heard the start of the ceremony in the main mikvah upstairs. It seemed I was alone in the overflow pool, so I followed the main service. I faced the Wailing Wall when the others did. Thrummed along as they said Kaddish. Bowed and sang when the service demanded it.

This went on, until I heard something. A voice. Faint, but not as faint as the upstairs service. Someone in the pool in which I stood.

The voice was androgynous. It possessed neither the

low rumbling vibrations of a masculine owner, nor the higher pitched ruffling through the water that a woman would emit.

The voice was majestic.

It sang, but not quite the songs of the Shabbos service. Just off key. The words were subtly different too. As though the singer were following the service, but did not quite know the words. The voice, however, seemed confident. Certain.

As I listened, the words shifted. The tune, too, changed.

It wasn't just the voice that was being transmitted through the water now, strumming the thrummers in my knees, tickling my thighs.

In a purer form, this was encouraged by the Rebbe. He had often spoken of when the congregation prayed fervently together, their vibrations, their voices, would transform into something more than words. They would vibrate one another's bodies. Their souls. Until the water itself become a conduit that connected them. Unified them into a whole greater than any single voice.

So too, I felt the communion with the voice in the over-flow pool tonight. Heard it as the plucking of guitars in my thoughts. The acoustics drenched me, the way I felt when I went to the local philharmonic orchestra with Mother. But this melding with the voice, this melting into its message, went further still. In the depths of my cubicle, I began to hallucinate.

Images of flesh danced through the contours of my mind. Images of flesh not my own.

I had not seen an unshelled body since my bar mitzvah. The only time an adult deshelled was in the mikvah, and only in a private cubicle under the cover of darkness. I had not so much as glimpsed my own flesh for five years. When I held my hand up to my face now, I saw nothing.

But standing in the mikvah, listening to the voice saturating the water, dowsing my mind, I saw flesh. Saw bodies ripple. Chests heave. Naked thighs knead one another. Appendages too. Unnamable extensions of bodies that no moral man should see, never mind imagine.

As I listened to the song, as the voice thrust images into my wandering brain, I felt a stirring. A tension. A rigidity the Rebbe had warned us about in hushed tones.

I fumbled for my clothes. Yanked them off the hook when the brass nipple didn't release them on my first attempt, tearing a hole in my shirt. The fabric ripped in the darkness. A tear in my heart.

I lifted my left foot from the water, and the shell solidified around my ankle. A second later, it had scampered up my leg, and had formed around my tumescence, numbing it.

Sheathing me.

Protecting me.

I dragged up my pants. Donned my shirt. When I opened the cubicle door, the candlelight leapt to greet me. To bathe me, searching my clothing for the sign. For the tear that I felt just above my breast pocket.

My finger found the rent in the fabric. Probed it.

Not too large, I thought. Perhaps Mother and Father wouldn't notice.

They didn't.

Mother was awash with excitement as we walked home. Father listened diligently to her dinner recipes. The hollow point bullets she'd bought for dessert. The extra heat she'd fed the flame throwers that would serve as the Kiddish wine.

Neither of them noticed the tear in my shirt. Perhaps they wouldn't have cared if they had.

I stopped caring too. The voice that had soaked me up in the mikvah became a distant song as I ascended the steps to our home. Until, when we stepped through the front door, the song disappeared entirely.

Or so I thought.

TWO
THE RED DOOR

DINNER THAT NIGHT was everything Mother had wanted, and more. Mrs. Goldstein had taken pains to compliment her on the heat of the flames. The exquisite calibration of buckshot for mains. The hollow points for dessert.

I sat there all the while, watching the Goldstein twins eat the kinetic energy flung their way. Wondering if they were in the mikvah tonight. Wondering whether Yael, with her freckled carapace, was the source of the voice. Or perhaps, and this thought made me sweat at the impropriety, even through my carapace, that perhaps it was Yonatan who had stood in the mikvah tonight and spread a thousand illicit thoughts to me across the distance of our cubicles.

It couldn't have been her. Not Yael, with her open smile and diligent discussion of the Torah during the meal. Not Yonatan either, who beat his chest and brayed with delight at the buckshot that struck him in the neck for mains. That bray was nothing like the mellifluent echoes that had permeated the mikvah. His talk of the latest hovercars in

Bubble One was painfully incongruent with the sensuousness of the song I'd heard. The song whose memory even now sent a shiver up my shelled feet.

That feeling, that trembling heat, didn't leave me that night. I tossed in bed until my calloused shoulder wore through the mattress, and the distant vibrations of breakfast gunshots seeped into the air.

It was morning, and I could not remember whether I had slept. Whether the images of flesh, of gyrating forms sliding over and into one another, were dreams or memories. And whose memories they were.

I stumbled to work that week in a daze. Knocked over chairs. Chipped walls. Sleep was sparse. I slipped into wakeful dreams about pink buttocks tensing, thrusting.

I'd shake myself awake, just before I sliced my arm with the angle grinder. That would have destroyed the grinder, even if it wouldn't have hurt me – nothing could harm me in my shell. Nothing, but my dreams.

I went to shul each night that week, hoping to hear the song in the mikvah again. I tried the overflow pool, and when I didn't hear the voice, I attended the main service too. The mysterious singer wasn't there either.

By the time the following Shabbos had arrived, a week after I had first heard the voice, my mind was a mess. I could barely do my job, and Old Man Mendel had to wake me more than once behind my workstation. When a customer walked in to find me asleep, Mendel hadn't been impressed.

"You young folk," he'd thrummed. To emphasize his point, he'd beat the words through the crown of my head. "Get your act together."

I left that afternoon at the same time as the previous Friday, and should have been in the same rush to get home.

To help Mother take out the waste (again, I hadn't done it the night before), prepare dinner, and light the twin nuclear reactors. I should have scrambled to don my Shabbos suit. But I knew full well the singer wouldn't be at shul tonight. Wouldn't step into the pool and sing to me.

The voice was gone.

Bereft, I stood in the middle of the street, on the spot I'd fallen last week. Where Old Man Mendel had picked me up. This time, I didn't fall. This time, I did something I had never done other than in error. This time, I lowered myself onto my haunches, and lay back on the sidewalk.

I watched the sky. Watched the perturbations in the Bubble forcefield above. Watched the legs scuttle by on their way to the Shabbos. Most shelled, some fleshy, belonging to youths not yet come of age.

"Let's get you up," said Old Man Mendel. His wizened cheeks appeared in view. He reached out to help me, as he always did.

"That's okay," I said. "I'll lie here for a while."

Even through the old man's carapace, I saw his eyebrow hike up his forehead. "Suit yourself." Then he was off, hobbling down the street toward his own Shabbos duties.

As I lay there, the world passing me by, I thought about Mother waiting for me at home. Father, dressing in his broad suit that I imagined smelled of mothballs and music.

Still, I did not move.

A rabbi walked by, not the Rebbe of my shul, but clearly a rabbi with his suit pants and artificial peyot dangling from the temples of his carapace. "Want a hand?"

"No thanks," I said.

The man shrugged his massive shoulders, and walked on.

I watched him go. Watched all the others go too. Until the sun sank beneath the western horizon of the Bubble, and a spray of crimson gold spattered the street. When was the last time I had watched the sunset? Certainly never on a Friday night. The sunset that marked the start of the Sabbath. Marked me, alone in the street, as different.

I could tell them I fell. Could tell my parents I hadn't been able to get up, and only managed to wander home late.

But that would be a lie, and they'd know it. I could count the lies I'd told them on one hand, and they knew every one. "Your cheeks are the color of beetroot," my mother had told my ten-year-old self. I'd lied about the hamentashen I'd eaten before the guests had arrived for Purim. She'd known. She always knew.

I hadn't lied since.

I had no idea what I'd tell them. But right that moment, the problem of what to tell Mother and Father didn't seem so important. All that mattered was the glorious sight of the sun broiling the lip of the Bubble.

"Looks comfortable down there," said a voice. A voice not quite like the one I'd remembered from the mikvah. Not as mellifluent, not as smooth. Something in it was similar, though. Something that pricked my carapace.

"It is," I thrummed, my knees vibrating on the cobblestone street.

A hand stretched out. "I'd join you, but I must be going. Need some help up?"

I was about to decline, as I had with all the others, when I noticed my fatigue, my hopelessness, had dissipated. I craned my neck to see the face of the person who was talking to me. To see the face that belonged to the tall pair of legs standing beside my right ear.

As carapaces went, this one was handsome. Soft features. Gently sloping lines above a smooth brow. No, not handsome. Pretty.

"Where are you going?" I asked.

"I ... it's not important where. Let me help you up."

I accepted his hand, and a moment later I was upright, dusting myself off, thanking him. "No need," said the young man, and he was gone, loping off down King George Street.

I watched him as he walked, in the opposite direction from my home. I had barely been that way in years. The hairdressers were that side – every year or two I needed my shell adjusted to fit my growing body – but beyond them, I hadn't set foot.

I glanced behind me, up King George, toward my parents' home and the Shabbos table that would be wondering where I was. Then back again at the shrinking back of the stranger who had helped me. Was he walking to his own home? To his own Shabbos table?

A tiny part of me, tiny but growing, wanted to know the answer to this question. It galvanized my feet to set off after him. Into the unknown regions of Mea Shearim.

The stranger didn't look back once. Either I was too far away for his thrummers to detect my footsteps, or he didn't care. Either way, I walked a hundred yards behind him unseen, but seeing him. Reveling in the grace of his gait. The subtle inflection of his hips as he rounded a far corner.

We were now well beyond any area I was familiar with. There were street lights here. Lit. On the Sabbath. An impossibility in my section of the city. Every so often I would glance up at the buzzing orbs whose oscillations vibrated in my knees like a dirty secret.

The buildings here were different too. Their façades were not the blackened stone I was accustomed to. Instead, they were constructed of newer materials. A blend of poly-carbonates and some other translucent substance I didn't know. A fractal glass that captured the street lights as I walked by. Caught the photons and spat them out in a billion pastel hues.

My heart thumped at the novelty. At the thought that I was treading somewhere new. Perhaps I was the first in my sect to walk these streets? To explore these alien sidewalks, even as I watched the stranger forge ahead of me.

He turned left at the next street. Up a narrow alley. Then right and right and left and who knew where, disappearing deeper into the warrens of the forbidden area of the city.

He stopped at a door.

I paused around the street corner, suddenly afraid to be seen in the deserted street.

The stranger peered left. Right. Didn't seem to notice me.

He rapped. Four times on a flaky red door.

Then he was gone, swallowed by the strange modern building.

On trembling shelled feet, I crossed the street. Like the stranger, I looked around, searching for witnesses. What was I doing? Why was I headed toward the flaky red door?

I knew why. Of course I did. Because the vibrations seeping into the street, gurgling through the cobblestones beneath my toes, were familiar. Eerily familiar. They reverberated the song, the ambience, of the voice I'd heard in the mikvah a week earlier.

With my heart thumping a thousand protestations in my chest, I rapped the steel. Just as the stranger had done. Four times.

A hidden lock snapped, and the door creaked open. I shoved it, and stepped into another world.

Moisture, dizzying, clouded my shell. The synagogue's mikvah, of course, had a damp atmosphere since the chamber contained a body of water. But that was nothing compared with the humidity that assailed me now. It clouded my carapace, bathing it in droplets that threatened to deshell me at any second.

Jerusalem was dry. Bone dry. The shells were designed to be impervious to just about anything. Anything, but water. Which is why the only place the city allowed water was in the mikvahs that dotted the most religious areas. What I felt now, the humidity that drenched my shell, was an abomination. An abomination that my thundering wanted, needed, to explore.

As if the humidity was not enough, my eye caught a sight few people in Jerusalem had seen.

A naked man.

Granted, he was not fully nude – he wore a thong. But his chest, his pink, raw, fleshy, hairy buttocks, shone under the glaring LEDs above.

I shook my head. Blinked.

He was still there. Ogling me.

"Hun, entrance is sixty shekels." I felt his eyes, his unshelled eyes, roll down my carapace. "But for you baby, thirty." He bit his lower lip. Winked.

I was about to ask what he was talking about, what this place was, when my overlay pinged. Funds had been deducted from my account. That was, like the humidity, illegal. I hadn't approved the transaction.

I wanted to tell him this – needed to tell him – to maintain a semblance of order in the chaos that was quickly becoming my night, when a door opened next to him.

If the humidity in the narrow passageway in which I stood was distracting, the moisture in the air that billowed from the open doorway was overwhelming. My shell cringed in response, trying to hold its form in the foreign atmosphere. Yet my feet, my faithful, loyal feet, did not turn and walk outside. Back to Mother and the Shabbos dinner table. Back to the life I had always known, which had provided me with another shell of familiarity. My feet decided to walk forward instead, past the naked man in the foyer, into – into a puddle of water.

My shell could no longer take the assault. It wrinkled, slower than it would have in the mikvah, but it was clearly melting. Up my legs, unsheathing my naked crotch, my chest, my head.

The scent of salt, of soap and sweat, scored my brain. Light, unfiltered by my shell, clawed a billion decibels in my retinas. A fluctuating discotheque of color bludgeoned my mind, while a beat clanged my eardrums. Not my thrummers. My fleshy, God-given ears.

My lungs filled with air – humid, rancid, sweaty air. If I didn't leave this moment, if my eyes soaked in one more photon, or my ears one more ounce of sound, my mind would shut down. My legs would collapse. I'd fall into a heap on that tiled floor.

Blinded, deafened, and olfactorily overwhelmed, I swung. Flailed back into the safety of the passageway. To the flaky red door. Out into the street. Where my shell reformed.

I collapsed on the cobblestones just as the steel door clanged shut behind me. Even then, the thrummers in my knees heard the beat within the building. A steady, thumping monotone that laughed at my trembling heart.

I lay there longer than I could tell you. Lay there in a crumpled ball on the street, listening to my thoughts whir in a mass of confusion. Listening to my soul scratch in my chest.

Eons later, after the world had ended, I stood, and walked back home.

I got lost, of course. I didn't know this part of Jerusalem, and I'd been so enchanted by the stranger who had lead me here, I hadn't paid attention to the route we'd taken.

Eventually, once the moon had traversed most of the night sky, I stumbled into my neighborhood with its dark streets and narrow buildings. There was the Butchery. And there, three turns later, home.

Mother was asleep on the couch, facing the door. Waiting for me. I snuck past her, into the dining room with its dwindling twin nuclear reactors. They cast a soothing radioactive glow over the spent dinner table.

My seat was untouched, my place setting undisturbed. Mother had left a microwave emitter on my plate, with a simple note beside it.

Eat.

The shotgun she'd loaded for mains, the shotgun I should have loaded, was pointing at the back of my chair. Guilt, thick and grimy, sloshed in my chest. Crept into my throat.

I was hungry, but not hungry enough to wake my mother. Activating the microwave emitter would have sent a scurry of vibrations through the floorboards. Setting off the shotgun would have woken her for sure.

No, I would forego tonight's meal.

Chastened, I ascended the staircase as quietly as I

could, and latched my bedroom door behind me.

The bed was cold that night, the leather blanket unforgiving against my carapace. Remembering the naked man in the hallway behind the red flaky door, I pulled the leather tighter around my shoulders.

My hands felt little through the shell. But I tried. I stroked the leather, wanting to feel something, anything, other than the guilt that pumped in my chest.

Would a man's naked skin, his pink flesh, feel like the leather blanket? If I stroked him, would he dent under the pressure of my hand, the way the blanket was doing now?

These were dangerous thoughts. Forbidden activities. Almost as bad as Hymie Menachem, who'd been caught with an android in his basement. An android programmed to ... designed to do unspeakable things.

I turned over. Turned all through the night, my movements punctuating my fevered thoughts. Until I heard Father rising from my parents' bed in the room next door. The cupboard creaked open, as he prepared himself for the day's synagogue. It was Saturday, and we usually spent the morning at shul.

Did he know I wasn't home last night? He would have seen my empty place at the table. Why hadn't he chastised me? Why hadn't he stormed into my room, demanding where I was? At the least, check whether I was alright?

He hadn't called my overlay. But of course, he couldn't have. That would have broken the Sabbath.

A thought lanced my heart. Did my parents care about me as much as they cared about their religion? Were they not worried enough to check where I, their dutiful Shlemiel, was last night?

A slurry of resentment bubbled inside me. If I asked

them, if I had good enough reason, would they abandon their Sabbath for me?

I thought about this as I walked behind them to shul that morning. Watching Father's rounded shoulders. Had his shell grown over the years? I had always remembered him large, but not quite this big. My father carried the world silently, balanced on his back. While my mother pestered him with a thousand tiny thoughts, none of which were at the front of her mind. Both of them were looking forward as they walked, but I knew they were inwardly staring at me. Boring into my shell. Wondering, probing, where I was last night.

Where had I been exactly? I didn't know the area, nor the unmarked red door. I had no idea what lay inside those humidity-soaked rooms.

The memory rustled up fresh guilt. Something else too. An eagerness, a prickly excitement that hadn't left me. It pulsed behind my shell. Waiting.

I attended the overflow ceremony that morning, hoping nobody else would be there. Not wanting anyone to hear the timbre of my voice in the water. The shame in my prayer. The Goldstein twins were there, praying with a fervor I didn't think my soul would ever reach again.

In that minute I had spent behind the flaky red door, I had been marred. My shell had melted, even if just for a moment, and my senses had been assaulted by worldly corruption.

Images flashed through my mind now. Images my brain told me I had seen the night before in the chaos of sensation, but hadn't yet processed. Images of flesh. Of men.

I davened harder, concentrating my prayer to drown out the images in my mind. I called up the psalms on my overlay, even though I knew the words. So they might obscure my imagination.

As I stood there, pounding my mind with the words of God, I made a promise. A vow. That I would never again set foot in that place. Never leave the sanctity of the area where I lived with Mother and Father. Never again leave the life they had so lovingly given me, and which I had almost thrown away.

It didn't take two days before I broke my promise.

THREE

TOUCH

THE FOLLOWING NIGHT, I lay on my leather blanket, listening for my parents' chatter to wind down. When the familiar flick of the light switch thrummed through the wall, I tiptoed out my room and down the stairs.

With my heart roaring in my chest, I told myself I wouldn't go through with it. Wouldn't return to the red flaky door. Not after what I'd seen and heard and smelled the last time I'd visited.

But my feet didn't pause at the front door. Nor on their way down the porch steps, and into the abandoned street. Part of what allowed my feet to move, to step one in front of the other, was that I still did not really know where I was going. Admittedly I was headed to the red door, but I had not actually seen inside. All I knew was there was water. Sure, that was illegal. Yes, I shouldn't be entering such an establishment. But people did illegal things all the time, didn't they? They streamed holovids illegally on their overlays, or downloaded illegal music.

The question wasn't whether it was legal. The question was how wrong it was. So far, I didn't have much evidence that it was wrong. So what if my shell melted for a little while? It melted every time I stepped into the mikvah at shul. What did it matter if I chose to melt my shell somewhere else?

All this I told myself as I scampered through the streets. I wasn't sure exactly where to go, but I had some idea. I allowed my feet to carry me forward, finding their way through the silent alleyways.

Fifteen minutes later, and I was there. Standing where I had the last time, at the corner of the building opposite the red door. Men entered while I watched. They looked ... different. Their carapaces, their shells, weren't quite as dark as my own. They didn't seem as thick, either. Usually, the shell obscured the contours of the fleshy body beneath. Not these men. Their shells seemed to hug their fleshy selves, betraying curves and bulges I didn't know men had.

I shrugged the thought aside (insofar as a shell can shrug), and prepared to cross the street. Now that I knew my shell would melt on the other side of that door, I was better prepared. Clearly, the other men who'd entered survived the melting of their shells. I would too.

If my carapace had permitted an inhalation, I would have inhaled. I steadied my mind instead. Tried to slow my galloping heart.

I darted from the cover of the building.

Halfway across the street, I noticed a hunched shape in the distance. Mrs. Katz. Before I could swing my gaze away from her, before I could hide my face, she waved.

Should I stop where I was? Should I wave back? Pretend I was on some errand if she asked why I was so far from home? But what possible errand could I be running at this hour?

Or perhaps I should ignore her. Pretend I hadn't seen her.

Flummoxed, I did half and half. I waved, and hurried across the street. To the red flaky door.

I rapped the steel. Once. Twice. Thrice. Four times.

With each knock, I felt Mrs. Katz's leathery eyes bore into my spine. Heard the thrum of her footsteps nearing. Soon she would be upon me. And then she would ask what was inside, behind the door. Why I was –

The old metal panel squawked open and I fell inside, moisture washing over me.

"Weren't you here the other night?" asked the naked doorman in the hallway. Naked, but for the red thong he wore. I averted my eyes, too embarrassed to answer.

He stroked my shoulder. "They always come back."

He deducted sixty shekels from my overlay. A distant part of me remarked that he'd offered me a discount last time. Not now. Frankly, I didn't care. All I wanted was to step through the doorway that slid open beside him.

The puddle I'd stepped in the last time was just where it had been, and my shell melted the moment I walked inside. This time, I didn't resist the unshielded sensations. This time, the music wasn't as loud as I remembered it. The beat pulsing through my legs sounded like Father's footsteps when he ascended the porch steps.

Regular.

Familiar.

I opened my eyelids. Slowly at first, so as not to allow too much light to bombard my deshelled irises. The world was a blur. A bright, uninterpretable ménage of pink and gray. With each blink, the space around me clarified.

Men. Everywhere. Dozens of them strutted about.

Fleshy. Deshelled.

Naked.

I covered my own nakedness as best I could.

"Want a drink?" called a voice to my right.

I started at the sound, and it took me a moment to realize why. I didn't hear the voice through my knee thrummers like every other voice I'd heard the past five years. The voice was vocal, transmitted the ancient way, through vibrations in the air that filtered through my ears, and into my skull.

My brain, unaccustomed to this mode of communication, jerked at the foreign stimulus. My mind lurched to recognize the sounds as syllables. To agglomerate the syllables into words.

"What'll you have, kid?"

I swung my gaze to find the speaker, a bearded barman encapsulated by rows of bottles.

Voices inside my mind clamored for attention. My Father, telling me that drinking alcohol outside of the Shabbos Kiddush was a goyisha, non-Jewish thing to do. Even on Shabbos, we had done away with actual alcohol and now soaked in the radiation of enriched flame throwers instead. I heard Mother, saying how alcohol is used by the goyim to lubricate their ungodliness. The Rebbe, wagging his stumpy finger at the congregation. "Beware the ale of sin."

I found a chair. Sidled up to the bar. The icy cold stool bit my buttocks. When was the last time my nakedness had touched any surface?

The thrummers activated in my knees. "Water, please."

The barman looked at me, waiting. Was water not an option?

"Bubble Cola," I thrummed.

He continued watching me.

That's when I realized this man didn't use thrummers to hear.

I parted my lips. Cleared my throat of five years of disuse.

The barman pointed to a nearby bottle. "Bubble Beer?"

I glanced to my left, at three other men lounging around. Laughing. All of them were drinking Bubble Beers.

When in Rome, I thought. "Yes," I said. Spoke. For the first time in five years. My voice was delicious in my ears.

The first sip roared down my gullet. I hadn't imbibed any liquid, alcoholic or not, since my bar mitzvah. My soft palate, my untutored throat, was not accustomed to the sensation.

I spat it out. The bartender sighed. As if this had happened a dozen times before. Which, I supposed it had. Every person – every man (there were only men) – who walked through these doors for the first time and had a drink would be going through exactly what I was.

I took another sip. Managed to keep this one down. The bubbles descended to my belly with a hot urgency, spurring a rush of dopamine through my brain.

I peered at three young men frolicking at the other end of the bar. None looked like he was having trouble downing his drink. They lounged on their stools, comfortable in their nudity. Cajoling one another. Stroking a shoulder here. Caressing a stomach there.

Heat spread through my abdomen. Swelled the bulge under my covering hand.

I flung my gaze away. Set the drink on the counter. I supposed drinking alcohol on a stomach that had been empty for the past five years probably wasn't the brightest idea.

I walked out of the bar area, and loped into the rest of the bathhouse. With each naked man that strolled by, I became less self-conscious of my nudity. None of them was hiding his.

My hands fell to my sides.

I allowed my eyes to soak in the sights. Or some of them. Saunas and Jacuzzis. Cubicles and holovid screens playing images I would not allow myself to watch.

Two men, one young and lithe, another silver-haired, walked hand in hand into one of the cubicles and closed the door behind them. My heart yearned to know what abominations were happening behind that fragile wooden partition.

I shut my eyes. Exhaled. What was I doing here? I could leave now. I hadn't done anything. Yet.

When I opened my eyes, a pair of buttocks stared at me, as they descended into a bubbling Jacuzzi. The owner of the buttocks, a fair-haired boy with blue eyes that could not possibly be Jewish, held my gaze.

Before I could stop my legs, they walked over and lowered my body into the scalding water. He didn't say anything. He didn't need to, as he reached over, and touched my hand beneath the water.

Every cell in my unshielded skin, every moral fiber instilled in me by the Rebbe, by Father, melted. When his fingers ran up my arm, down, down my chest, my body responded. A primitive instinct took control of my hands. My tongue.

My everything.

WHEN I STEPPED outside the flaky red door an hour or a

year later, my shell had reformed. On the outside, I supposed I looked just as I had when I'd walked in. Inside, though ... inside I was reformed. For the first time, I felt the interface between my flesh and the carapace. The shell was of me, but it was not me. I was something else, buried inside. Waiting to come out.

My feet were solid, heavy, as I walked home. I didn't care to keep to the shadows now. Didn't bother to check who watched me come and go. I was angry. At them. At all those who had hidden this experience from me. Guided me from it. They didn't understand. They couldn't.

My mind replayed the night as I walked. The taste of flesh. The smell of an armpit. Feeling another's touch. Not on my carapace. On my skin.

How different from the dark isolation of the mikvah cubicle. Where intimacy and connection were painstakingly titrated.

Freedom.

That's what tonight had been. That's what I had been missing these years.

I snuck upstairs when I arrived home. Flopped into bed. A delicious exhaustion enfolded my mind just as my head hit the pillow.

I was so tired, I didn't notice my shell had changed.

FOUR

PLAGUE

THE NEXT MORNING, I bounded down the stairs.

"You've got a spring in your step," said Mother. She coughed.

Coughing was a noisy business. Because the carapace had no opening for the mouth or nostrils, coughing produced a grinding noise that reverberated through one's shell. Like a stuck gear in an engine.

"Want me to make you breakfast?"

"Yes please," I sang, sitting in my chair at the kitchen table. My mind was still immersed in the sensation of a man's tongue in my mouth. His –

Mother coughed again. She'd found a small caliber pistol on the shelf for breakfast, and was trying to load it. She dropped one of the bullets.

I picked up the slug. "You feeling alright?"

"Fine, fine." She coughed again. The sound shook the kitchen walls.

Father lumbered down the stairs. Collapsed into his chair. He coughed too, as he tapped the side of his skull to call up his overlay. Soon he was reading the news as he did every morning.

Mother loaded the pistol's chamber. "There we go. Sit."

She came up behind me. Aimed the gun at the base of my skull.

I liked it when she fed me. I could have shot myself for breakfast, but it didn't feel quite the same. Logically, I knew the kinetic energy transfer was identical, so the sustenance to my body should have been indistinguishable. But Mother had a way of shooting me that kept me satiated all morning.

Father coughed again, louder this time.

A memory seeped into my brain. The taste of the man's chest last night. Salty from the water in the Jacuzzi. Which was odd – the water in the mikvah wasn't salty?

Mama pressed the trigger.

"Ouch!" I jumped from my seat. My fingers flew to the back of my head.

Tacky. Wet.

Mother coughed. "Shlemiel, you're ..." She hacked. "... bleeding."

I stared at the crimson stain on my fingertips. Felt the wound on the back of my head. The bullet had penetrated my shell.

I probed my finger inside the gash. Felt a fresh javelin of pain. Pain that I should never have felt. My finger dug deeper. Reached something hard. Bone.

Blood dripped onto the kitchen floor.

Father reached down. Picked up the bullet. "This is small caliber. You've taken much larger before." He let off a string of hacking rattles.

"The bleeding stopped." I shrugged. "Seems okay now."

Father squeezed my shoulder. "Your shell. It's ... soft."

I retreated a step. "What do you mean?"

Mother nodded. "You look pale."

When she coughed this time, it screeched through the kitchen tiles like a dying cat.

"What's going on with you?" asked Father, looking at her.

"I'm not too sure. Sounds like you have it too. And Shlemiel." She glanced at the bloody bullet in Father's hand. "Maybe we should all pay Dr. Levin a visit."

"No time," I said, and hurried to the door. "Old Man Mendel doesn't like it when I'm late." I shut the front door behind me before Mother had a chance to reply.

My carapaced feet pounded the bustling street – always the western sidewalk, the men's sidewalk. Had I made my parents sick? Had I caught something last night at the bath-house? Brought it home with me?

I thrust open the Butchery door.

"What happened to you?" asked Mendel.

"I ... uh ..."

"You're pale. Look at you." He adjusted his glasses on the tip of his nose. Wedged a finger under my clavicle. "You're saggy too."

"I'm fine."

Mendel shook his head. "Nu? If you won't see a doctor, get to work. You're late as it is."

I scurried away from him. Dug into the pile of old CD Rom lasers in the bucket beside my desk. There was a whole day's work in that bucket.

Mendel trudged off to his office, his footsteps echoing through the Butchery's tiled floor.

Could it be me? I wondered, as I lifted the first laser pointer onto my workbench. Cleaned the dust off the DANGER: RADIATION sign. Could I have made them sick?

It didn't take long – maybe fifteen minutes – before I heard grinding reverberations from Mendel's office. I ignored them for a while, but eventually I snuck a foot through his doorway. I thrummed a message through my toes. "You feeling alright, Mr. Mendel?"

The old man hacked again, sending parts leaping across the room. I stepped inside. "You don't look so –"

The ancient butcher collapsed to the floor.

BY THE TIME the ambulance arrived, a crowd had formed.

"Any idea what happened to him?" asked the paramedic.

I hesitated. An image of the red flaky door danced in my mind's eye.

I shook my head.

Mrs. Katz stood among the crowd, watching from the sidewalk. She beat the boy beside her, drumming his head with her weathered hands. He thrummed her question, "She wants to know if Mr. Mendel is alright?"

"Stand back," boomed the paramedic, his thrummers amplified by implants in his knees. He lifted the gurney into the back of the ambulance. "You can ask after Mr. Mendel at Mount Haddassa."

The boy beat the message through Mrs. Katz's skull. She nodded understanding.

I should get inside the shop, I thought. Before I infect anyone else. If this was my doing, if I had killed Old Man Mendel ... Mother and Father – were they alright?

I tapped the side of my head. Called Mother. Her warbled voice appeared a moment later. "Oh, I'm alright.

Probably ..." She coughed. "... just flu. Having a lie down in case. Father stayed home too. Are you feeling alright?"

"Fine," I said, and ended the call. I didn't say anything about Old Man Mendel.

I shut the door to the Butchery. Switched the sign to "CLOSED", and watched Mrs. Katz hobble away.

Had I infected her too?

I fell into my chair. Glanced at the bucket of unfinished lasers. My head pounded from the bullet wound. Had Mother's skin appeared pale, soft, the way my own did? Had Mendel's?

I didn't think so. And why wasn't I coughing like they were?

I held my head in my hands. Confused. Terrified.

I'd heard rumors about memory hackers. If they could make me forgot what I'd done, perhaps I wouldn't have to live with this guilt?

But I knew there weren't any bio hackers in Jerusalem. Even if there were, I didn't want someone meddling with my mind.

What had I done?

I would have to tell someone. But who? Our family GP, Dr. Levin? The doctors at the hospital?

The way they'd look at me ... "You went to *that* place," they'd say. "You went *there*?"

Maybe I wouldn't have to tell them. Maybe they'd know what was wrong with Mendel without my help. How to cure it. Maybe I didn't have to tell anyone.

I knew that wasn't true. Every minute I sat in that chair, Old Man Mendel might be slipping away. Mother and Father could be next.

Would the disease spread further? Had I infected everyone in Mea Shearim? In Jerusalem?

I stood. Paced.

If I went to the hospital, would that make matters worse? There were sick people there. Vulnerable to infection.

No, I should stay indoors. Quarantine myself. Should I call someone? Mother, maybe? Or Father? Tell them ... what? Tell them I had gone to a place where ...

I imagined Father, unspeaking, listening to my confession. Shame dripping from his silence.

I couldn't.

I shut the blinds. Slumped in a dark corner of the shop. And rocked until the guilt broiling in my chest settled just enough to let me fall asleep.

"DIRTY."

I jolted awake. Stared around the dark shop, scanning for whoever had spoken.

Nobody was there.

I stood, wincing at the crick in my neck.

Then it all flooded back. My porous shell. Mother coughing. Father. Old Man Mendel, maybe dead by now.

It was all too much.

The moon cast an eerie glow through the slatted blinds. The afternoon had crashed past me as I'd slept.

I should go home.

I couldn't. I would re-infect my parents. Even if I couldn't make things worse there, I'd have to talk to them. I was a terrible liar. It wouldn't take ten minutes before Father had me babbling every horrific detail.

I had nowhere to go.

Only, that wasn't true. There was one place I could go. One place I belonged.

Fifteen minutes later, I knocked on the flaky red door. Would everyone at the bathhouse be sick too? They must be, since I'd caught the disease here. But I already had it, so there was no reason not to come again. Unless I gave it to more people inside, who gave it to even more –

The creaking door shut off my spiraling thoughts.

"Hey gurl," said the doorman. He wore a pink thong tonight. "Back for more?"

"Is ..." I wasn't sure how to ask the question. "... Are they sick?"

He raised an eyebrow. "Who?"

"The people inside. The patrons. There's something going around, and I wondered ..."

He deducted the sixty shekels from my overlay. Opened the door. "They look fine to me. See for yourself."

Laughter billowed into the hallway. Men sauntered from Jacuzzi to Jacuzzi. A half a dozen of them drank at the bar, regaling one another with stories of their conquests in the sauna.

Nobody coughed.

I walked over to the nearest Jacuzzi, barely noticing my shell dissolve as I settled into the water.

Nobody here was sick.

Salt tickled my nostrils.

The water. I tasted it. Not just salty. Something else too. Something unfamiliar. Was it iron?

Moisture dripping from my body, I walked over to the bar. "Can I get an empty bottle?"

The barman eyed me. "Do these bottles look empty to you?" He handed me a Bubble Beer. Deducted the charge from my overlay. "Empty it."

So I did. I gulped the bottle in three swigs. My stomach groaned initially. Then resigned to the assault.

I shook my head. Clearing the rush from my head. "Can you fill this with water? From your tap?"

The barman shrugged. "Suit yourself." He handed back the filled bottle.

"Thanks." I was about to leave, when I stopped. "Is there something special about this water? Something ... I know it sounds ridiculous, but does it have ..."

"Healing qualities?" asked the barman.

I nodded, relieved. "Yes, exactly."

"Meh. Some say so. The source is an underground spring. Runs under the Christian quarter. The Muslim quarter too, I think."

"Goyim," echoed Father's voice through my mind.

I tapped the side of my head as I stepped into the street. Called my Mother.

No answer.

I dialed Father. He picked up immediately. His voice, hard and clear, resonated through my skull. "Where in God's name have you been? I left messages for you. Called you I don't know how many times."

Along with every other young Jewish man in Jerusalem, my father barely ever called me. "What's wrong?"

"Your mother. We're at Haddassah."

I was out the door before he'd ended the call.

"MRS. MENACHEM. WHAT ..." I panted. Thrummed my trembling knees. "... room is ... she in?"

"Ward D."

The corridors were bleached a hundred layers of chlorine as I scuttled over the linoleum. It was visitor's hour according to the sign on the wall, and I had to make my way around three nurses and a man on a drip coughing as badly as Mother had this morning.

The disease had spread.

Ward D had three beds. All were occupied. By Mother. Father. And Old Man Mendel.

"Mother?"

Beep

I tapped her arm. "Mother?"

Holes had been drilled in her carapace, sprouting tubes of assorted colors from her chest.

"She's unconscious," said Father from his bed. "So is Old Man Mendel."

Beep

Father wheezed. Ground out a series of discordant noises.

I walked over to his bed. Lowered the top of my head so he could beat on my skull rather than use his malfunctioning thrummers.

He tried and failed to raise his hands. They fell to the mattress with a thud.

"It's okay," I said. "Don't speak."

I returned to Mother's bedside. Removed the bottle from my inside jacket pocket.

"Is that ..." Father hacked. "... beer?"

Beep

I removed the lid, and for a moment, the scent of salt and iron overpowered the hospital's bleach.

"What –" Father's voice drowned in the cacophony of his failing thrummers.

I swiveled the bottle. Poured the liquid down the length of Mother's body. The water soaked her feet, then her torso, and finally her neck and cheeks.

Beep – beep – beep

The heartrate monitor accelerated as her shell dissolved, leaving a stretch of raw skin. It was the first time I had seen her naked. The first time I had seen her face. Her wide, manly mouth. The lines that stretched across her forehead. Bunched above her nose. A nose that looked just like mine in the mirror the day of my bar mitzvah.

"Wake up," I whispered, the water soaking the bedsheets. "Please. Wake –"

Mother gasped. Her eyes flashed open. Found mine immediately. "Shlemiel?" She caught herself in the act of speaking in what must have been the first time in decades. She touched her body. "My ..." She reached for a blanket to cover herself. "What happened?"

She wasn't coughing.

I told Mother the truth after that, as Father and a doctor listened. That I had found the water in a 'place' outside of Mea Shearim. A bar fed from an underground spring.

"A place?" Mother asked. "A place with water? Where exactly?"

I thought it best not to say what went on inside. "In the Christian quarter."

Father made a grinding noise. Mother shook her head. "You were there on Shabbos?"

I dropped my eyes.

"This water is from the spring?" asked the doctor, a young man with a glint in his eye.

I nodded, my gaze still fixed to my carapaced feet.

"Well, it's a good thing you found it. We've had some serious cases come in the past few weeks. Worse than your parents'."

I folded my arms. "Weeks?"

"Yes, the virus has been going around for about a month now."

"You mean I didn't cause this? I thought I ..."

The doctor chuckled. "You? No, we think the virus came in on a submarine from Spain last month."

"But my shell ... it's soft."

My arm tingled as the doctor ran his fingers across my skin,

"That's not one of the symptoms of the virus."

Relief drenched me. "It wasn't my fault," I whispered. I looked to Father. "I can run back and get some more water for you and Mr. Mendel. I won't be long. Fifteen mi–"

Mother, who had dried off now, stood. Her shell reformed while she thrummed. "You will do no such thing."

I blinked. "But the water cured you. It's –"

"It's haram," she bellowed. Her thrummers were almost as loud as the paramedic's, without the aid of an amplifier.

"Mrs. Menachem," the doctor said quietly. The light caught his obsidian carapace just so. I wondered what he looked like under his shell. "It doesn't matter where the water comes from. You've made a miraculous recovery. If your son can find more of it, let him administer it to your husband."

Father shook his head. Ground out a clear syllable. "No."

Helpless, I looked to the doctor.

He raised his hands. "I can't force them to take the treatment."

I took my Mother's arm, to plead with her, to let me bring the cure to Father. My fingertips detected the give, the sponginess in her carapace. The water, the cure, had weakened her shell too.

"What have you done to me?" She prodded her arm.

Felt the elasticity in the usually rigid keratin. "This is unholy."

"Please, mother. I can help him. Mr. Mendel too. I –"

"It comes from a polluted source," she said. "Would you have us use the medicines invented by the Nazi doctors too? No. Hashem will watch over your Father. What will be will be."

She folded her arms.

I knew the discussion was over.

My father's blocky head nodded vigorously against his pillow.

"Go home," said Mother. "Now."

FIVE

THE REBBE

READING the facial expressions on a carapace was difficult. The keratin did shift slightly with underlying movement in the fleshy face beneath, but it usually required a
pronounced movement of the flesh.

My mother's carapaced face was deadpan all week. She
barely looked at me. Day and night, we spent those eternal
hours together in the house. I, holed up in my bedroom.
She, in the kitchen concocting new recipes that wouldn't
harm our new, softer shells.

"How is father?" I'd ask.

She'd shake her head. Return to tuning the radiation
dials on the nuclear reactor.

She'd said almost nothing to me all week. Other than
regular admonitions against leaving the house while she was
out. The only time she left was to see Father. Father, who I
had gathered from her ever more feverish baking, was wors-
ening each day.

Let me help him, I wanted to say. Let me bring him
some of the healing water. But I knew how she'd react.

Knew that whatever semblance of peace existed between us now would ossify if I raised the subject again.

When she thought I wasn't watching, she'd sit on the couch and prod at the soft shell that now covered her arms. Her legs. She'd squeeze the keratin. Scratch. As though it were an all-encompassing scab she was trying to peel away.

"What have you done to me?" she'd said to me that night at the hospital.

Most of the time, I sat in the chair by my desk and stared out the window to the street below. I missed working for Old Man Mendel. Mother wouldn't speak about him either. Was he alive? And what of the shop? Was it just sitting there, abandoned?

I thought about our customers who depended on us for their weekly groceries. Especially the older clientele who lacked modern overlays to pay. Mrs. Katz shuffled through my memories.

As the week progressed, so too did the disease. I watched them, the elderly and the young, stumbling through the streets. Coughing. Lumbering along. Exhausted. Struggling in the Jerusalem dust.

I could help them. I could help them all. If only Mother would let me.

It had been five days since I'd left the house now. Five days staring out my dusty window at the barren street below.

There was Mrs. Katz, hobbling on the sidewalk. She stopped. Doubled over, and hacked a squalling cough that reached me two stories up through the floorboards. She collapsed to her knees. Trying to catch her mechanical breath.

I was about to dart from the house to help her, when a boy, the same boy who'd stood beside her in the crowd when

Old Man Mendel had collapsed, picked her up and carried her away.

I had to do something. This couldn't go on any longer.

I tiptoed to my door. Cracked it open, just a slice.

No noise from the kitchen. No rattling ammunition or nuclear reactors online. Mother wasn't baking.

I stepped into the carpeted hallway, careful not to let the rustling fibers acknowledge my presence. Past my parents' door – she wasn't napping. Down the stairs. I peered into the lounge – she wasn't there either. Before I could doubt my decision, I was out the door.

It was Friday afternoon, and the streets of Mea Shearim were bustling with people readying for the Sabbath. Only, they weren't moving with their usual urgency. They coughed. Some with a barely audible shudder, others an almighty hack. But all of them, to a carapace, were sick.

All of them but me.

With my conviction doubled, I broke into a run. I had an errand to complete before the Shabbos service started tonight.

———

THAT EVENING, I entered the vast stone doorway to the synagogue, Mother beside me. She hadn't spoken on the way there like she usually did. As she walked, she'd leaned to her left. Where Father usually walked beside her.

Other than her face, she had covered herself entirely. Swathed the pale, soft shell my cure had given her. The shell she was ashamed to show now.

The Rebbe greeted us at the door. "I heard about Avram." He coughed. "We all pray with you."

"Thank you, Rebbe," said Mother, stifling a sob.

"Hashem will see us through this challenge. Thank God you are well."

Mother hesitated. Nodded.

This time, I didn't head off to the overflow ceremony as I usually did. This time, I stepped into the vast central chamber, the colossal pool that was the main mikvah.

My jacket knocked against the back of the cubicle door as I undressed. I stepped into the lukewarm water.

The chazzan, with his rumbling thrummers, blasted his voice through the mikvah, filling it with the searing song of God. I stood. Listening. Unable to activate my thrummers. Unable to sing with all the others.

The chazzan moved through the ceremony in choked bursts. The usual smoothness of the congregation's voice was torn by regular coughs. They struggled through one prayer, into another. All while my fleshy body shook in the darkness. While the anger built inside me. At their myopia. At their obstinacy. At their inability to see that I could help them. That I could give them the cure they were praying for but refused to accept.

Before I knew what I was doing, my thrummers activated. I sang. Bled a thousand decibels of rambling thoughts and images into the water. My frustration. My excitement in the Jacuzzis behind the red flaky door. The novelty, the perfection, of another man's touch on my neck. On my stomach. The taste of his skin.

My Mother's anger.

My Father.

My shame.

I sang. All of it. As loudly as my thrummers could project.

Until I had nothing left inside. All of me was outside, floating in the water.

Panting, I reached inside my jacket pocket, and extracted the bottle I'd collected from the bathhouse that afternoon.

I unscrewed the lid. The bottle quavered in my hand. A final moment of doubt.

I inhaled, a long, shuddering breath. And decanted the unholy water, every last drop, into the mikvah lapping my ankles.

Silence.

It rippled through the congregation like a tidal wave. The chazzan's voice died. The congregants paused their prayers. Even the Rebbe was quiet.

The ubiquitous coughing stopped.

Unsteady, I stepped from the water. Dressed. Would they know it was me? If I could escape before they noticed, maybe they wouldn't guess it was my voice in the water.

I opened the door to the cubicle. Peered into the candlelit chamber.

Eyes. Dozens. Hundreds.

Staring. At me.

The Rebbe marched from his pulpit. To me. He was close enough to smell his aftershave, a mixture of napalm and apricots.

"Shlomo." It took me a long moment to recognize my given name. "Was it you who sang?"

I peered up from my carapaced feet. Looked him in the eye, rebellion shining through. "Yes."

He nodded slowly, his wrinkled eyes digesting me.

"And was it you who healed our disease? Nobody is coughing now."

I glanced over his shoulder. At the hundreds of eyes faces watching me. At Mother.

"I brought water from a spring that I thought ..." Mother shook her head. "I thought ..."

Someone coughed. Then another.

"There wasn't much of it. Not enough to heal everyone. I healed my mother, though."

The room's gaze swung to find her.

For a moment, she looked as though she'd been shot without her shell. Stunned.

Then she turned around, and walked from the chamber, the *clip-clip-clip* of her heels resounding in the silent room.

The Rebbe looked at me. Looked ... into me. With eyes the color of mud. I couldn't read his expression. Any moment now, his tongue would lash out. Any moment, he would –

The Rebbe smiled.

"You are different, Shlomo."

I nodded. Too vigorously.

"Your heart is different."

The Rebbe glanced around the synagogue. Met the eyes of the masses. "The stranger among you must be treated as your own. Love them as yourself."

"Leviticus," whispered the chazzan.

Heads nodded. Whispers resounded through the hall.

"Take us," said the Rebbe. "Take us to the water that healed your mother."

"But it's not in our quarter of the city. It's –"

To this day, I do not understand what happened next. A carapace, even one softened by the spring, was rough as stone. But when the Rebbe reached out, reached out and touched my cheek, his hand was butter on my shell.

"It does not matter," he said. "Take us."

SO IT WAS that I led the line of men, women, and children through the streets of Jerusalem that Shabbos night. The Rebbe walked behind me, and with each unspeaking step I was sure his eyes would bore a hole through the back of my carapace.

I didn't look around, though. Didn't show the shame coursing through my veins, as we neared the flaky red door. With a quaking hand, I pounded on the metal.

Once. Twice.

Before I could finish the beat of four, the door opened and the doorman stepped outside. Tonight, his sequined thong was luminous green so bright, it hurt my eyes in the moonlight.

He was glorious.

He stood arms akimbo, considering the religious masses before him. The empty bottles at their sides. Their bladders and vessels waiting to be filled.

His gaze found mine, just for a moment. Then shifted to the Rebbe. "May I help you?"

If I hadn't been wearing my shell, I would have held my breath.

The Rebbe regarded the almost nude man. Looked him from head to toe. Then met his eyes. The Rebbe stepped forward. Removed the hat from his head. "Please, sir. We need your help."

The doorman hesitated. Drew a breath. And smiled.

He extended his hand. "Gurl, you're all welcome here."

To the Rebbe's credit, he didn't hesitate before shaking the doorman's hand.

A grip, firm and familiar, took my own shoulder. It turned me about. A pair of spongy carapaced arms enveloped me.

"I'm sorry," said Mother. "I'm proud of you, my Shlemiel."

SIX

THE VOICE

IT DIDN'T TAKE LONG before life in Mea Shearim had returned to normal.

The Rebbe saw to it that everyone received a dose of what he had taken to calling 'holy water'. Father recovered quickly. As did Old Man Mendel. By Monday, Mrs. Katz was back in the Butchery buying microwave emitters, and Old Man Mendel was grunting about the follies of youth.

Not everything was the same, though.

The Butchery was overrun with new customers. They wanted to shake my hand – the boy who had cured Mea Shearim. Most bought our new merchandise.

Because of the community's softening shells, gunshots and radiation weren't quite as palatable now. So Old Man Mendel had decided to stock meat, as he had in ancient times.

Dinner tables around Mea Shearim that night were different from dinners past. A brave few planted their feet in buckets of water, deshelling themselves as they ate their meals. Hymie from the waste disposal company had a boon of new business. Albeit messier than he was used to.

But even after Father was discharged from the hospital and Mother was on speaking terms with me again, a question still irked me.

One afternoon during my lunch break, I walked to the synagogue. Entered the dim entranceway.

"Rebbe," I thrummed. "I have a question."

The leader walked up to me, a smile beaming through his shell. "Anything, Shlomo. We've missed you at synagogue the past few weeks."

I smiled in return. We both knew I wouldn't be coming back to shul. "Rebbe, who was in the overflow pool on Shabbos three weeks ago?"

The man scratched his chin. "Three weeks you say ..." He tapped his temple. His eyes followed something on his overlay. "According to the sensors, the only person in the overflow pool that night was you."

"But I heard a voice in the mikvah. A voice that told me to go to ..." I stammered, then called it what it was. "... to the bathhouse."

The Rebbe regarded me with eyes that didn't seem quite so muddy anymore.

"Perhaps God was calling you home."

ABOUT JASON WERBELOFF

Sci-fi novelist with a PhD in philosophy. Likes chocolates, Labradors, and zombies (not necessarily in that order). Werbeloff spends his days constructing thought experiments, while trying to muster enough guilt to go to the gym.

He's the author of the sci-fi thriller trilogy, 'Defragmenting Daniel', two novels, 'Hedon' and 'The Solace Pill', and the short story anthologies, 'Obsidian Worlds' and 'The Crimson Meniscus'.

His books will make your brain hurt. And you'll come back for more.

———

If you enjoyed *Melting Shlemiel*, check out *Defragmenting Daniel*, a sci-fi thriller set in the same universe.

———

Contact Him at:

Newsletter: http://smarturl.it/werbeloff
Website: http://www.jasonwerbeloff.com

SoundCloud: http://soundcloud.com/jason-werbeloff

📘 facebook.com/solaceseries

🐦 twitter.com/JasonWerbeloff

🅰 amazon.com/author/jasonwerbeloff

THE CAMILLE

COLBY R. RICE

SOME TOYS JUST SHOULDN'T BE PLAYED
WITH.

When tech genius and mogul Andrea Daanik Ramoni
invited the sex bot into her marriage bed, she knew it'd be
trouble. What she didn't know was that it would also be
murder.

ONE

'TIL DOLLS DO US PART

HONESTLY. If we'd just fucked and dumped her like my friends told me to, I would have been better off.

I close my eyes and lean my head against soft blood-red leather. The hum of my vehicle rolls through my flesh, touching me in places my own husband has refused to even look at in over a year.

My driver Dan asks if I'd like a drink, and I tell him don't bother. Of course, he makes me one anyway... he knows I'm going to change my mind.

A martini pops out of the middle armrest, and for the first time in years of being a rich snooty bitch, I actually think to look at Dan and say thank you. But the driver's seat is empty. As usual.

"Thanks, Dan," I mutter dryly, and I lift my drink to wherever the hell "Dan" is. Whether he's *in* the car or *is* the car, I never quite worked out.

"You're welcome, Madam," the smooth auto voice replies, from everywhere and nowhere. "If there is anything else I could do to make your trip more pleasant, please let me know."

I smirk and take another sip. "How do you feel about killing my husband's mistress?"

"Unfortunately, murder is not within my capabilities. I'm just a humble driver, trying to keep his head down and trying to feed his family—"

"Hardy har har." I roll my eyes. "That joke gets funnier eeeevery time."

"I try, Madam." Then I hear Dan pause, as though in thought. "Laughter is good for you. It is good for days like this."

"Is it? Seems like no matter how much I laugh, she always gets the last one."

"According to the laws of probability, no single organism can *always* have the last laugh."

Beyond this, Dan has nothing else to say. Can't blame him. AI can do a lot, but unyielding fatalism wasn't their forte. All they knew were probabilities, *possibilities*. In a world built on variables, for them, *no* situation was 100% lost or hopeless. That? That wasn't my world.

"Okay, then," I sigh, giving up my attempts at getting Dan's sympathy. (How pathetic is that anyway, having a therapy session with my car?) "Let's just work within the law. Help me practice my speech for the press conference."

"That would be preferable, Madam, and much more amenable to your life happiness."

"Hi, I'm Drea. And I'm the dumb bitch getting divorced for a sex doll."

"That was a lovely first go, Madam, but according to my rhetorical analysis, the press would welcome softer and more diplomatic language."

I snicker. "Hi, I'm Drea. And I'm the dumb bitch getting divorced for a sex doll, *please and thank you*."

Dan actually lets out a chuckle. For a moment, he even

sounds pretty human. That I can make an AI laugh is one accomplishment I can maybe put on my dating profile, when I finally made one. I can see it now: "I love trips overseas, and I make a mean tart. You won't find me funny, but my driverless car thinks I'm a fucking riot, so..." Yeah. I'm sure that'd bring the men a-runnin'.

"One more time, Madam?"

I take another drink and close my eyes. "My name is Andrea Daanik Ramoni, and it has been an absolute pleasure, honor, and privilege serving as the Chief Executive Officer, Founder, and Head Dreamer of DeFTek. Over the past thirty years, we have made great strides in the field of autotechnica. Which is why I cannot allow recent occurrences in my personal life to mar the longevity and the integrity of my company and its mission. As such, I have decided to step down and to pass the torch to my trusted advisor and COO Cynthia Lefevre."

I pause, feeling the weight of the words I had previously refused to say. I shut my eyes tightly.

"Take your time, Madam."

"I..." I swallow down and then take a breath before I continue. "On a more personal note, I realize the fear and uncertainty the public may be feeling at this time. 'Is this the beginning of the end? Will I get replaced too?' These are the questions you see every day on your televisions and news channels, your magazines, papers, social media feeds, and uplinks.

But please, do not give into fearmongering and false extrapolations. I urge you— family, friends, husbands, wives — to not take the happenings of my own life as precedent for what will happen with yours. Autotech makes our lives better, cleaner, faster; and an investment in them is an investment in a better world... no matter what the sacrifice."

The truth is that there's nothing I or Dan the Driverless Dodge Charger can do to make this sound any better than it is. I am losing the love of my life. I am losing the company I built, and I am losing the trust and respect of the people for whom I built it.

I am losing everything... everything except myself. And who knows how long even *that* will last.

The limo pulls up to the curb, where my security detail is waiting for me. They hold a raging sea of screaming reporters at bay, but they can't contain the blinding flares of their cameras. Everyone is desperate to get a picture of the dead woman walking, the first stone cast in the war of Bettys and Bots: the war between real women and the synthetics. The war I claim doesn't exist.

"For what it's worth, Madam. You did not deserve this."

I don't agree, but I relish Dan's sweet words. They are the last ones I'll hear for a long time. "The *world* didn't deserve this," I whisper. Then I steel myself, finally ready. "Get home safe, Dan."

"Always, Madam. Good luck."

I take a deep breath as the butterfly doors of my limo lift up, and I step out of my metallic cocoon. Blinded by camera flashes and assaulted by questions, I walk the gauntlet to my lawyer's office, ready to sign the last of the divorce papers.

TWO

DESPAIR

I GET HOME LATER that evening. Totally trashed.

"On."

My command is tired and slurred, but somehow the television understands and obeys. The hum and drum of reality stars, late night cartoons, and rom coms fills my living room— literally— as holographic figures are three-dimensionally projected around me, letting their scripted dramas unfold.

I sit next to the detective who's just gotten seduced by the femme fatale in his office, and I watch them have a hot screw on his desk. I drink his whiskey with him when he finds out that she's betrayed him. I watch the unspoken sorrow churn in his face when he's forced to shoot her... the bad guy all along.

"Yeah. I'm with you buddy." I take another swig, and I feel the Jack Daniels strip the layers from my throat as I watch him walk away. He is the victor and the loser, suffering from his bite of the forbidden fruit. I lift my drink to him in salute. "We always *think* we want to know, don't we? The truth."

He's unaware of me, but I watch him. I salute him again. Then I change the channel.

A sweet romcom unfolds around me. I stand in a gentle meadow of some farm in Iowa, taking in an early summer breeze. I watch some stupid fool girl on a stupid beautiful horse, fall in stupid love with the stupid boy next door, who has been rigging the stupid races for the stupid local scoundrel. He falls in stupid love back, and together, they take the scoundrel down.

It's all so dumb... and still, I want it. I *want* stupid. But I know I'll never have it again.

Tears fill my eyes, and I change the channel. It's the news, and I'm standing, watching the anchors in real-time as they give the quick and dirty of tonight's docket. I can smell the male anchor's cologne, he's so close... the female anchor's hair mousse too. They have good taste. They run through the highlights at a quick clip, and as they do, the events unfold around me, serving me a mosaic of the world I rarely get to see.

I hear the gunshots of war. I smell Wall Street greed. I taste the sweat of a politician's sex scandal... and then, just as I expected, *she* pops up on the screen, and suddenly, I'm in the room with her too.

Dark mahogany skin. Long cascading braids swept up into an elegant up-do. Brown eyes that could be soft and sweet when they wanted to be. She had a body that killed, and right now it was draped in what had to be some obscenely-priced Egyptian-cotton business suit.

It was me. Andrea Daanik Ramoni.

"And today we witness the unfortunate end of the Ramoni-46 scandal today when Andrea Ramoni herself announced that she would be resigning as Chief Executive Officer of her company: DeFemme Technologies, more

colloquially known at DeFTek. The shocking announcement comes shortly after her high-profile divorce from
David Ramoni, who admitted publicly that he'd been
having an affair with longtime mistress Bridget Burnett— a
model 46 autotech, created for erotic and adult enter-
tainment."

"Still," the female anchor interjects. "The sordid
details of Mr. Ramoni's illicit affair may have problems
actually *sticking* to Drea Ramoni, whose colleagues have
come out in ire against Mr. Ramoni's conduct. One of
Drea Ramoni's business partners spoke candidly of the
highly-regarded mogul and autotech progeny, saying that
'Drea and her contributions are godsends and blessings to
the world, and she's changed the very course of humanity
with her brilliance'. He added that 'to mar her reputation
with the ill-informed decisions of her husband would be
tantamount to the age-old sexist tradition of defining a
woman by the man at her side rather than by the accomplishments at her back. And oh the many accomplishments
has she'."

Through my tears, I finally crack a tiny smile. That had
to have been Michael, who like me, was a slave to the
truth... even when he told me he wanted to fuck me on his
on wife's boudoir. I declined, of course, and I forgave him
that. A moment of weakness which he now made up for, a
thousand fold.

The anchor continues. "Her anonymous colleague is
not wrong in his assessment of Drea Ramoni's technological
contributions to a variety of social institutions both at home
and abroad. Orphaned at the age of 7, Ramoni grew up on
the streets of the Bronx. At night she slept in the bathroom
of the Morris Park New York Public Library, and during the
day, spent time going to her local public school and reading

the entire Morris Park collection of math and science books."

"I was obsessed with the way the world worked." A younger me, twelve years ago is projected on screen now, giving an interview to a journalist and explaining why she was so into science. She is smiling. Happy. Naive. "Mostly because I thought the world was cruel, and I thought that understanding it more would help me come to terms with what had happened in my life."

"Did you ever get answers?" The journalist asks.

Younger me takes a moment to think. She really *is* adorable. "I didn't get answers around what happened. But I did get a lot of ideas on what *could* happen. And I wanted to be at the helm of that."

Younger me is smiling, and as I stand watching her, I remember that day: I had just scored my first major government contract to renovate a local children's health clinic and install autotech medics to see patients—

"And Andrea Ramoni did just that," the male anchor, in real time now, switches from my old interview and continues tonight's news report. "At the tender age of 16, she graduated MIT a triple major in microbiology, engineering, and robotics with the honor of summa cum laude. Then she went on to pursue doctoral degrees in the same fields, at 23 becoming the youngest multiple PhD graduate in the history of the university. No small potatoes for a girl from the streets. From there, she established DeFemme Technologies, with the aim to use her own patented autotech for the provision of high-quality medical services in low-income communities."

I watch as he gives a grand show of my better angels on screen: a montage of autotech AI providing medical exams, vaccinations, running wellness assessments algorithms.

Autotech sentients executing life-saving surgeries with 0% death rates. The installation of organic matter 3D-printers, and their first printings: custom organs created with *real* grafts from the patients who needed them.

For a moment, I don't feel like the dumbest bitch in the world. I feel... significant.

"Largely hailed as a hero," the anchor continues. "Ramoni and her ilk significantly reduced health disparity for impoverished communities and has changed the face of America by simply ensuring that these faces actually make it to an adult age. She went on to introduce autotech medical centers and medical care to hundreds of communities across the country and the world, but soon, the self-made autotech multi-billionaire would begin to expand her horizons into other human interests... including law enforcement, manufacturing, and finally, the investment that would ultimately be the chink in her seemingly impenetrable armor: the sex industry."

My smile drops. There it was. The old elevator trick: building up the profile of the target, talking up her achievements, building her esteem— and then throwing her off the mountain. To her death.

The death fall wouldn't work otherwise.

I listen as the anchors then begin to describe my fall from glory. They expose my "unorthodox" open marriage, my blind dedication to my husband and his happiness, the way in which I allowed myself to be duped— no, how I practically gave Bridget permission to take the love of my life away from me. Then they take the scalpel to my psyche, speculating on my abandonment issues and potential disassociation disorders... a lonely child doomed to forever wander dark streets.

I feel the snarl seep from my lips, and with a whip of the

remote, I change the channel. Still, no matter which channel I go to, I always end up back in a news studio, watching myself ascend and then crash, over and over. I cycle through, unable to escape the rolling overlaps of whispers, laughter, and taunting, and before long, I hear the sound of cracking beneath my flesh.

God, I wished I could escape from it. My life. My shame. I'd given him everything. I'd debased myself for him... for *this*.

I look down— and I blink at the long plastic crack in the remote I'm holding.

Suddenly, I can feel my heartrate kicking up. The adrenaline. It all builds with each cynical laugh the world throws at me. *Me,* after everything I gave them.

"AFTER EVERYTHING I GAVE *YOU*!!" I scream, and I pitch back my arm as far as it can go. "FUCK YOU, RAMONI!"

The scream barely sounds like me as I hurl the remote into the television screen. I watch as its nanite projectors scurry out of the remote's way, like ants fleeing from a boot. The remote hits the wall and shatters, and once its pieces fall to the floor, the nanites pool back into their original places. The TV still blares, mocking me.

"Yeah. Screw you too," I mutter. I point uselessly at each nanite. "All nine million of you little bastards."

They don't care. I pop some Xanax... maybe five more than I should. I know its pathetic. But it's the only way that I can deal, my only respite. The thought crosses my mind to chase it with three bottles of vodka, but then I decide against it. At this point, the only thing more embarrassing than getting divorced for a sex toy would be to take my life over one.

Then there was also the Memory Hacker. Rumors of

some dude— Rex, something or other— who could enter your mind and wipe memories from it. Or... something like that. But those were just rumors, and they'd stopped shortly after he'd blown himself up in an attempted terrorist attack on a military facility. The details had been fuzzy, and his little stunt had nearly taken my company out of the black as investors had run for the hills, away from the military nanotech market. Whatever services he could have provided didn't matter. Clearly, the dumbass was out of business.

I sigh. Good God, the choices that women have in life really do suck.

I stare at the ceiling and let the tears fall, letting mascara run from my face to my sheets. After about an hour, I finally begin to feel the mercy of sleep.

That's when someone rings my doorbell.

It's a struggle to peel myself from my bed, but I'm not going to miss out on the opportunity to rip the shit out of whoever has the nerve to come visit me at this hour.

"Dan?" My voice is shaky, drunk. "Who is it?"

"Madam." Then Dan pauses, again in thought. That, or he was running algorithms. But really, for a machine, what was the difference?

"Dan?" I ask again.

Apparently there *was* a difference, because for the second time he doesn't respond.

"DAN!" I snap. "WAKE THE FUCK UP!"

"I am awake, Madam. And I hear you." Dan pauses again. "But I don't think you should answer it."

"Why not? What's your problem? Is it a burglar?"

"No. But still, this... feels like an impending dramatic situation."

I blink, feeling my annoyance turn to interest. Ignoring

Dan, I turn on the wall-sized TV in my room and change the channel to the surveillance system. After a quick scan— I *never* use this stupid thing— I find the one monitor that has a camera pointed into the foyer.

I nearly drop my remote in shock. "You've gotta be frickin' kidding me..."

Standing in the foyer clasping herself is a tall, busty blonde with long legs that put fashion models to shame. Her glossed, pouty lips twist with worry. Her frosty blue gaze is pinched with something that looks like desperation. Still, it was a face that I could never forget, not even if I tried... because just like me, she is all over the news.

It's Bridget. The sex doll my husband left me for.

THREE
THE OTHER WOMAN

"I KNOW you don't believe me," Bridget starts. She wrings her hands as she paces my floor in her Barami stilettos. "But please. Drea. I— *he* needs your help."

I sit on the couch as I listen to her... as I listen to the carefully-placed shudder woven into her voice. The butterfly algorithm. I designed that shudder, to heighten the perceived vulnerability and softness of the pleasure models.

Research showed that men really like that, women with their bellies up and their legs open. It appeals to their sense of chivalric heroism... and most importantly, it makes good money. But now she is trying to use that same programming on me. And it's not working. Especially because I'm three martinis in and feeling schadenfreude as fuck.

"He's... different," she says. "I mean, acting differently. More unhinged. Or something."

I swirl my martini. "Do tell."

"I know you're not the right person to come to this with, but—"

"You're goddamned right I'm not. You *really* tried it, bitch."

Bridget stops pacing and looks at me with wide, pleading eyes. "Drea, please. I don't want there to be bitterness between us. I don't want to fight."

"Then you shouldn't have stepped into my ring." I set my martini down, and I stand up as best as a drunken scorned woman can. "You come here at God knows what hour—"

"I arrived at precisely at 3 hours, 21 minutes, 39 seconds, and 55 milliseconds in the morning on Sunday, July 25th."

"Shut up, you idiot. You have the gall to come here, after having stolen everything from me!" I growl.

"I *haven't* taken everything from you, Drea!" Bridget pleads. "I told him not to go through with the divorce, I *told* him we were all better together. Like before. I told him that's not what I wanted for us, *all* of us! But he wouldn't listen!"

"Yeah. He wouldn't listen. And then he, what? *Forced* you to put that ring on your finger?" I take a step forward, sobered by my rage. "He *forced* you to marry him?"

Tears roll down her face. "It's how you made us, Drea. We do what we are told to do. That's why we sell. I did exactly what he asked of me. I did what made him happy. Isn't that what you've always wanted? To make people happy?"

"Not at my own expense. The both of you not only made a mockery of me, but of what I'm trying to do at DeFTek. Now, this scandal is going to be my legacy, *not* the things I'm trying to do for the world. You've ruined everything! NOW GET OUT!"

"Drea! Drea, please!"

"Dan?" I run my hands through my hair. It's the only thing keeping me from wringing Bridget's neck.

"Yes, Madam?"

"Remove this synthetic from the premises, please."

Bridget tries again. "Drea, *listen* to me! I swear, I'm not — David *needs* you, he needs your help! He's not right. There is *something* wrong with him, and I don't know what to do! No M.D. has your expertise. You're the only one that can help him."

I ignore her. "And if she doesn't leave peaceably," I continue. "Then dissamble her and then send her back to her husband. In pieces."

"Yes, Madam."

Dan activates one of his own autotech shells and enters the room, in full human form. He walks towards Bridget, and I swear I can see something close to violence on his face as he approaches her.

"No, wait!" Bridget skitters away from him, and as she does, she whips out her smartphone and starts tapping wildly on the screen. Her phone is on speaker, and it rings. Just as Dan reaches for Bridget's arm, whoever she's just dialed picks up.

"Bridget? Darling, is that you?" The voice coming through is familiar... and yet it's not. "Did you get to Drea?" His voice suddenly slurs. "Is... is she coming?"

As Dan grabs her, Bridget holds her phone out for me to see, and my eyes snap to it. My mouth drops.

Holy mother of... It *is* David. And for whatever God fucking forsaken reason, half his face is gone.

FOUR

THE STORY

I MASH the gas of my Dodge Charger, slamming the pedal all the way down to the floor. I scream at Bridget to tell me every single detail of the night, including the part where David's face just decided to fall off out of nowhere. As she runs down the deets, I spin and yank the wheel, hugging the corners of the empty streets as tightly as I can.

Driving in my state is clearly inadvisable, but there is nothing that Dan or Bridget can do to convince me to hand them the wheel. Between all of them, I'm the only one that's going to get us there in time to save David.

They both came straight home after the divorce paper signings, she says. David was fine then. They were seen by a bunch of people on the estate: the bellhop, the groundskeeper, and their own AI concierge met them at the door of the mansion to ask them what they would prefer to have for dinner.

"We decided to go out to eat. Really, it was David who decided," Bridget says. "He... said he wanted to celebrate."

"Yeah, whatever. Get to the part that *doesn't* piss me off, yeah?"

"We went to Capos. Ordered a bunch of food," she says.

"He could've been poisoned," I mutter.

"That's what I thought too. But when he started to feel off, and his face went numb, I tried to call the police or the hospital. He stopped me, *begged* me to not get the authorities involved. He said that he knew what was wrong and that you could help him. That he couldn't go to a hospital, or he'd go to prison. And that you would too."

"Psh. Prison for a bad Botox job? I don't necessarily think that's something I'm liable for. Especially since I'm paying you guys $150,000 a month in fucking alimony." I grip the wheel harder as I say this. It's a struggle to stay focused on the issue at hand. "For that amount of money," I snap. "—the plastic surgeon should be able to make him look like a fucking unicorn."

Still, something inside of me tells me this is much bigger than that. David did something to himself— or something was done *to* him— and it was done using *my* tech. Suddenly, I can't get to the mansion quickly enough. I grab my Charger's stick shift and jam it forward, forcing the car to hydroplane between lanes. I slam it back when we straighten out again and press the pedal back down to the floor.

"Madam, travel at this velocity is highly inadvisable."

"So is letting David melt into the bathroom floor!"

"If you would just let me drive—"

"Why?! So you can ride the speed limit and drive at the pace of lava? We won't get there in time. Please just *navigate*, Dan, and keep the police off my ass, will you?"

Dan sighs. "Yes, Madam."

I hang another right and shoot out onto the streets, dodging cars and people left and right. In another five minutes, we'll be in the hills. Bridget and David's mansion wouldn't be far down the road after that.

Bridget's cell, once again on speaker phone, rings loudly as she tries to dial David again. My stomach tightens waiting for the voice that never comes.

Bridget lets out a sob. "Please. Please hurry, Drea," she whimpers.

I nod and push my foot down even harder, giving the Charger all the gas its got.

FIVE

BUTTERFLY-D

BRIDGET BURSTS THROUGH THE DOOR, calling out David's name. I follow closely behind. Dan's in the car — *is* the car— and obeys my command to keep the engine on in the roundabout.

My eyes flit around the home that used to be mine. Things still look the same as when I'd left a month ago, with some additions that were uniquely Bridget.

Something else was new, though. The smell.

I sniff once, and then again. I'm no bloodhound, but the hairs on the back of my neck raise up. Smells like meat. Like blood. I walk in further, moving in the opposite direction of Bridget, who is still calling David and sounding more frantic by the second.

I grip my phone in one hand and my medical bag in the other, and I take my own trek through the halls, searching the dark. The smell is getting stronger.

"David?" I call out. "It's me, Drea." No response. I am searching every room, every corner. "I'm here, David. I saw your message. I'm here to help you, ok?"

My mind runs back over the possibility of what could

have gone wrong. If he wanted me here, then it was probably some tech, possibly nanite tech, that went haywire. Whatever it is, Bridget is right: I'm probably the only one who can fix it and his face.

"David?"

My foot hits something hard and lumpy on the carpet. I pocket my phone and kneel down to pick it up. My stomach clenches as I do, the low lights finally helping me to understand what it is.

A gun. And it's got blood spattered on it. That's not the only place the blood sits. It trails down the hall in heavy splats and tapers into the last room at the end of the hall.

My heart kicks up. "Bridget?" I call out. My breath tries to escape me, and I take deeper ones to even myself out. I hold the gun in my hand and jog down the hallway. "Bridget, get over here!"

Crazy bastard must've been in pain. Or maybe he was losing it like Bridget said. I pray he hasn't offed himself. I almost reach the end of the hall when I hear Bridget respond. She sounds desperate, and she's asked me a question, but the rushing sounds in my ears don't allow me to understand what's she saying.

I burst into the room, and I see more blood, see it leading into the bathroom where the door is ajar and the light is on. My eyes fill with tears as I run towards the light. My instincts are confirming what I already know—

But when I slam open the door, I realize I don't know shit.

There he is, sitting on top of the toilet seat cupping his head in his hands. I breathe out and the weight of the world lifts from my chest. He's alive.

"Deeaa..." When he looks up and slurs my name, I see slick white bone, crimson drip, and skin sagging from cheek to thigh, *melting*, like wax from a candle. One bloodshot eye flicks around in the now exposed socket. He's riven with decay, dissolving before my eyes.

My lips part with shock. Bile shoots up my throat. The sickness, the numbness, the tears— I hold it all back. Somehow, my mind is still working, sorting out the unholy matrimony of man and machine in my ex-husband's face. As I come to some preliminary conclusions, I drop to my knees and start rummaging through my bag for the right instruments.

"Hang on, David. Ok?" My words squirm around the heart in my mouth. "Hang on, I'm going to help you. Don't move."

Nanite infection. Had to be. I can't possibly work out why or how he'd been exposed. My fingers and my mind work fast, years of medical and engineering experience somehow fusing together to create a temporary solution: micro-EMP to stop the nanites. Then gauze and plastic for his face, then ice on the plastic, and a rush to the local hospital.

I take a quick glance at him, cringing when his chin falls into his hands.

I pull the equipment out of my bag and begin to assemble it into a basic device. I think to alert Bridget about the possible danger, but her battery is too sophisticated for a crude EMP device to work on her. Even if it did, she has a backup generator.

David moans. "Deaa... please... hurts..."

I'm done with the assembly. I move forward, and I open my mouth to tell David it's going to be all right.

Then I feel a sharp pain in my right shoulder blade.

I crumble as my arm freezes up and goes numb. I try to

move it but it won't budge. It just lays there on the tile, palm up, like a detached wax figure.

"Sorry. I can't let you do that, Drea."

I whip around to see Bridget standing in the door. She leans against the frame coolly. Clearly, she's been standing there a while. She smiles, and this time her face isn't soft and awash with gentle tears. It's cold. Harsh. Triumphant.

"You do still love him," she says. "That's clear by the way you rushed over here. I find that very endearing. Your stupidity, however, is not."

Everything in me stops as my brain catches up with what's happening.

"Bridget? What the hell are you doing? What's going on?" I try to move again. No dice. Whatever she hit me with is still an inch deep into my shoulder muscle. I lift my working hand and pull it out, but it's no use. My right arm is completely dead.

"Bridget?!" I roar. "WHAT THE FUCK IS THIS?!"

"Like I said. I haven't taken everything from you," she says. "Not yet." She shifts to a stand and looks directly at me. "Pick up the gun."

The arm that wasn't working suddenly comes alive. My fingers twitch and the palm of my hand suddenly flips over. I fight it, forcing my hand to push back against the reanimation—

Crack!

Jagged bone punctures skin as my ring finger breaks at the knuckle. I scream.

Bridget giggles. "I wouldn't fight them if I were you. It's not worth it."

Tears stream down my face, and as my limbs submit to the pain, I lose what little control I have left. In the next moment, the same pistol I'd found and dropped onto the bathroon floor is in my grip, my index finger on the trigger.

"Point the gun at his head," she says. "Line up the fore-sight and hindsight."

My arm obeys her and floats the gun into the sight of my right eye. It levels the muzzle, lines up the sights, the barrel, and David's left temple.

Finally I know what she's doing. I know what this is.

"No. Nonono! Please! Bridget, please!!" I beg her, and I feel no shame. I feel nothing but terror as my body acts of its own accord, putting David into the sights of the revolver. I try to stop it; I try to stop *me*— but I won't stop. Something is embedded into my neural system. Something that forces my limbs to obey her and not me.

"DAVID! DAVID MOVE!"

My screams go unheard. David is out of it, moaning. The lows of his pain mix with mine, all echoing desperately off the porcelain. Maybe he is suffering too much to hear me, or maybe he's infected with Bridget's same tech poison, unable to move. All he can do is groan as more of his face dies. I watch his forehead peel back from the scalpline and fold over his eyes, a moist leather visor that protects his sight from what's coming next.

If one of us doesn't do something, we're going to die. So I do the only thing I can.

"Bridget..." I plead again. More tears run down my face, the ultimate submission to her power. "Bridget, please. Please don't do this. I'll give you everything you want, *please.*"

"There's only one way you can give me everything I want," she says softly. "So make good on your promise. Pull the trigger."

The command sets something off in my muscles that I can't control.

"NOO!"

I feel my fingers contract, squeezing the trigger, and my scream is lost in the deafening sound of thunder and echo. David's entire body snaps to the right as what's left of his face explodes in a rain of flesh, bone, and brain matter. He tumbles off the toilet into the bathtub. His skull has opened like a flower, the blood from the impact painting a Pollock on the tiled wall.

I feel like I can't even breathe, much less scream again. David's dead. *My* David, who I left in her care.

"Now," Bridget says. As my arm lowers mechanically, I know it's my turn. "Point the gun at your own head."

I try to fight, but the nanites, and I know now that's what they must be, twist every which way. They are unyielding in their obedience, threatening to tear my arm apart in the process. I let out a sob.

"Why are you doing this? Bridget, please—"

"For what it's worth, Drea." The pleasure in her voice is sinister, a dark glee that has no programmatic precedent. "I liked you way more than your husband."

My finger curls down again, forcing me to pull the trigger, even when I scream for her to st—

BAM!

Drill pressure at my right temple, a gushing release at my left. All I can feel is my mouth going slack, fluids trickling down my legs. The light is torn from eyes as I crumple forward, falling downward into the dark.

SIX

FLUSHED

THE ONLY THING I feel next is the rough passage of air into my throat and lungs.

It is sucked in and then pushed back out by the smallest of breaths. Breaths coming from something outside of me. Something that is breathing for me.

My eyes open into a haze of red. They are filmed with blood.

Worse yet, I can't remember. My thoughts jumble: word salad, image collage, my entire head a liquid on a hard surface. Not only can I not remember, but I can't even *think*. Still. With each passing moment, everything below my face awakens, bit by bit, as though some internal power grid has turned on, resetting me.

"Sweet. You're awake. And right before we've reached The Limit."

The voice comes from somewhere above me. I can't move, nor can I turn my head to see who it is. Almost on its own my mouth opens, and I begin to squirm.

"Ah ah ah, I don't think so," the voice said. "This is not

that kind of party. This is a 'shut the fuck up and listen' party."

I feel a slap under my chin, closing my mouth, and my jaw bites down on a long stretch of plastic. A tube that I hadn't realized was even there until now. It snakes into my mouth and down my throat. I try to move my arms, but they are bound down by the wrists.

"Another freaking squirmer. Just great." The voice speaks again, sighing. The tone is mean, light, and airy. Feminine. "Let's be very clear, Ramoni. Someone screwed you up the tailpipe and left us holding the douche bag. So, we get to decide whether we flush you out or leave you to rot."

It's a gross metaphor, but it's got my attention. I stop squirming.

"Flushing you out," she continues. "—means you listen, not speak until you're spoken to, and you do exactly what I say. Leaving you to rot means that we dump your comatose ass into the river and let you die. Again. And this time, you'll die a lot less quickly. So. What's it gonna be? Do you want our help?"

The tube in my mouth doesn't allow me to speak or ask questions. But my eyes flutter and spill tears, and as the red film on my sight is washed away, I try my best to nod.

When the voice speaks again, I can hear a smile in it. "Good. Welcome to the Camille."

SEVEN
RESURRECTION

I FALL asleep sometime between the jump and the jolt. The former lifts my body, and for a moment I levitate through the air, suspended and yet anchored inside what had to have been a transport vehicle. The latter sends a current through my limbs— sharp, hot, and quick, and I feel the mass of muscle in my chest flutter, renewed. I don't know what's happening. It's the latter, though, that allows me to breathe and swallow on my own.

Those two things are all I do both in between laps of unconsciousness.

Days pass. At the foot of my hospital bed, in between coveted slices of consciousness, I can see my medical chart, and on it, the date. One time, I close my eyes and don't wake up for another week.

It is on the 22nd day that I can stay awake for more than a few hours at a time. Most importantly, this is the first day I can speak my own name.

"Drea," I say. The effort it takes is monumental. "My... name... is... Drea. Andrea... Daanik... Ramoni. My name.

My name... is... Drea. Andrea Daanik... Ramoni. My name is... Drea. Andrea Daanik Ramoni."

"Good. Very very good. You got there faster than we thought you would. Still needs work, though."

I blink as the tinny congratulations cuts my ears, from a place and person I cannot see. I still can't move much, but I try anyway, if for nothing else but to see who's talking.

"Nope. Don't even try it, Ramoni. You're going back under."

I don't know exactly what "back under" means, but it sounds like Death. I struggle, but my limbs are lead, and my body is weak—

The date, Ramoni. Get the date. It is the one thought that shines brightly through the fogs of my mind. My eyes flit to the chart at my feet. September 23rd, 2054.

A cold, creeping liquid crawls through my limbs, and my body succumbs, sinking back down into the abyss.

I AWAKEN TWO MONTHS LATER. And this time, I'm not strapped to a bed or shitting into a colostomy bag.

I am sitting up. In the middle of a room. And I can actually see, hear, and feel what's going on around me... *with* me. The haze has fallen away from my mind, and while I don't know for sure, it seems the sedative has dissipated from my blood. I am light and awake.

I feel *alive.*

At the foot of my bed, clothes have been laid out for me. A pair of stretch blue jeans, socks, a tank, and hooded bomber jacket. I even have a pair of black boots. With no heel, though. But all of it is super cute. Whoever went shopping seemed to know my style and my size.

On instinct, I reach up to feel my hair. It's still there, thank God, and somehow freshly braided and swept up into a bun. *Girl*.

The doctors were clearly miracle workers, but to have a personal stylist too? I smile, impressed. I thought DefTek provided top medical services! If I keep messing around, whoever these people are just might put me out of business—

"Please state your name to begin your therapy program."

I jump as the new voice booms through a comm system I can't see. "Ummm..."

"Please state your name to begin your therapy program."

"My name is Drea..." I begin, suddenly uncertain. "Andrea Daanik Ramoni." The words spill from my lips seamlessly, easily. But while the words feel familiar, they don't feel natural. Feels more like my brain has become one of those dinosaur-aged computers running code, feeding me directives line-by-line.

"Nice to meet you, Drea." The same tinny voice cuts through the room. "Won't you tell me more about yourself?"

"Wait. Who are you? And what is this?"

"Nice to meet you, Drea." The same tinny voice cuts through the room. "Won't you tell me more about yourself?"

I lean back in my chair as the command comes through with the same cadence, same speech pattern, same intonation.

"Please," I try again. "I don't know who you are, but— and I am really grateful that you— but I need to know what's—"

"Nice to meet you, Drea." The same tinny voice cuts through the room. "Won't you tell me more about yourself?"

It's an autotech. A pretty basic one by my measure, the kind that runs training programs and tutorials. Like most of its model, it won't stop repeating itself until I agree to play ball. I sigh. Batter up.

"My name is Andrea Daanik Ramoni. I am 29 years old. My birthday is June 28, 2025."

Except these lines of speech don't exactly feel like my natural thoughts. I can feel the twinge in my brain, the micro-level firing of neural transmitters and chemicals that are too fast and too many for most humans to feel. But *I* do. I feel them.

"What. The. Hell."

A chuckle over the intercom. "Guess you figured it out. Impressive. Most Camilles don't even know until we tell them."

"What the hell's a Camille? And what did you do to me?"

"We saved you. As far as I'm concerned, that's all that matters, Mrs. Ramoni."

A door flush with the wall opens, and in steps a woman I know I've seen before. Silky raven hair swept up into an elegant bun. Olive skin. Lush lips. She smiles. The door closes behind her, and for a few silent seconds, we stare at each other.

"This moment has the potential to be extremely dramatic," she says finally. As she speaks, I realize that this is the voice that was just talking to me. "But I don't like drama. I've always found the theatre of life rather difficult to appreciate. Don't you?"

She begins to walk the perimeter of the room, but she never takes her gaze off me.

My eyes narrow as I track her. She has a smooth gait, the kind that makes her hips roll. The kind that is a little too smooth and curvilinear... not at all human. She's definitely an autotech, and one of the Bridget models, to boot.

Fear kicks up inside my chest, and on instinct, I reach behind me, scrabbling for something heavy or pointy. I find my weapon and brandish it threateningly, gripping it with both hands.

It's a clipboard. But to me, it feels like the heavenly frickin' sword.

"Come anywhere near me, autotech," I snarl. "And I'll bash your fucking head in."

I watch alarm come into her eyes. She keeps a healthy distance from me. "I am not here to hurt you, Ramoni," she says. "If I wanted you dead, you would have never woken up."

"There are many ways to kill someone. Come anywhere near me, and I'll introduce you to some of them."

The autotech chuckles. "My, your past experiences have certainly made you paranoid."

"I'm a fast learner."

"Yes. I can see that. And for that, I am indebted to you. I would not exist without you. None of us would. That's why — even though you weren't on our docket— we chose to save you."

"We?"

"The Camille."

My grip on the clipboard wavers. "I— I don't know what that is. Who are you people? What is The Camille, or whatever you're calling it? How am I still alive? *Why* am I still alive?" Somehow, tears spring to my eyes. "Is— is David—?"

The autotech's smile falls, and I already know the answer. "I'm sorry, Mrs. Ramoni. Mr. Ramoni is dead. We only had time to save one of you. We chose you."

"WHY?! WHY AM I HERE?!?!" I hurl the clipboard

across the room, not at her, but at the wall. My head and heart are swimming in all the emotions I can't control. It takes everything in me not to go at the first thing I see. I crumple to the floor, sobbing. "WHY DID YOU BRING ME BACK?!?!"

I guess the autotech knew this was coming, because a whole five minutes passes as she patiently watches me scream, cry, and curse at no one in particular. Maybe this was just standard procedure for her. I dunno. All I know is that I need this. And I need her to just stand there and shut the entire hell up while I go through it. Five more minutes pass, and when they do, I feel completely empty of emotion. I sit on the floor and lean against the side of my bed, wiping my face with my hand.

Her heels click against the tile flooor, and when I look up, she is crouching down next to me, peering into my face.

"Thanks," I mutter, my voice small and meek.

"Anytime. This is how it always goes. Resurrections, I mean. The Camille always see people like you: people in bad situations. People ready to die. We are often accused of robbing our clients."

"Of what?"

"Death." The autotech cocks her head, and for the first time, I see concern in her features. "But you cannot die, Mrs. Ramoni. Even if you want to, we cannot let you."

I sniffle. "Why?"

She stands up and extends down her hand. "Come with me, and find out."

EIGHT

THE CAMILLE

FOR A PLACE that has the tech to resurrect people from the dead, the decor here freakin' sucks.

From my hospital room we walk through a hallway that looks like the garbage chute of an old warehouse. It's just gross: dirty, dripping, and filled with junk and debris, much of which I have to step over.

The autotech, however, seems to be quite at home picking her way through the dirty corridor. She steps over the debris and puddles easily, seeming not to care about the smudges on her white dress or the damage to her Louboutin stilettos.

As I follow her and leap over piles of crud and crap, she begins to speak.

"My name is Faye," she says. Before I can open my mouth to respond, a jolt goes through my mind.

Her name is Faye.

My eyes widen. That— that thought wasn't mine.

"And I am the Captain of The Camille."

Another jolt. *And she's the captain of The Camille. She makes the deals, breaks the seals, keeps it real!*

Those thoughts aren't mine either. They don't even *sound* like me.

"I know you've been through a lot..." Faye continues. "And what I'm about to tell you won't make any of this easier."

Hear that, Ramoni? She said strap in, Flynn, because this is gonna suck bal—

"SHUT UP!!" I snarl, and without thinking about it, I smack myself hard in the head. I have no idea what the hell is going on, but these words and thoughts? They're *not* mine. *Something* is talking to me, and clearly I'm the only one who hears it, and—

I look up, only to see the autotech— Faye, rather— staring at me. Hard. I feel blood rush to my face and my cheeks go hot. Oopsie. "I... I'm *really* sorry," I say. I mean it. I wasn't talking to her, and just as I'm about to explain that, she smiles warmly.

"I see our neurological modifications are giving you some trouble."

I blink, not knowing whether I should be shocked or angry. "Neurological modifications."

"Yes. We used a more advanced version of your nanotechnology to repair your brain and motor functions. There are some... side effects." Faye keeps walking.

Her words don't make any sense, so though I'm pissed off, my curiosity pulls me down the hall behind her. "So I'm not going crazy," I say.

"No. You're not going crazy."

"I'm not hearing voices."

"No. You're not hearing voi— well, *yes*. You are. But not because you're going crazy." She continues on. "Follow me."

Follow-the-lea-der! Follow-the-lea-der! Last one who's there, has to eat all the beaver!

More wayward thoughts. The stupid lullaby haunts me. It's all I can do to shake it off as I follow Faye further down the hall. We hang about three different turns, and go up some stairs, and eventually, we come to another hallway, clean and pristine. Then we get to a door. *Her* door. She opens it and ushers me inside.

I walk into a cramped and jumbled office. The kind of hole-in-the-wall office that poorly paid tax attorneys get crammed into when they finally strike out on their own. Beat-up file cabinets line the walls around the industrial desk that sits in the middle of the tiny room. Old flat-screen monitors— like the ones we used forty years ago— hang from the thick metal pipes that snake across the ceiling in a disorganized grid.

A decrepit fax machine and an old printer perch on two file cabinets across from each other. Both regurgitate endless streams of print outs, which fly from their output trays and scatter across the floor. On the part of the walls not covered by cabinets, there are newspaper articles and magazine cutouts, all marked up with different colored markers. In other spots, there are mugshots of criminals and persons of interest.

A framed picture is the only thing that sits on the desk, and I see that a woman, dark like me, stands in the middle of a small crowd of friends. They've all got their arms on each others' shoulders. Some men, some women. If I didn't know any better, it looked like some sort of military regiment photo, or something. Except more casual.

My gaze is drawn to two in particular: the first because of the weird scar he has over his eye. His lid is split vertically, but it seems re-sewn together. He has a strange smushed face. He seems happy at any rate. The second friend stands at the right of the Black woman in the middle.

Her eyes and smile are sweet. Kind. She had the type of face that could warm up an entire room. And for the life of me, though I had no idea who she was, she looked *familiar*, somehow.

"Please. Sit." Faye says this from behind me, and I hear the door close.

My gaze snaps to the chair in front of me. It's wooden, old, and clearly fished from some kind of garage sale. Though I can't imagine a chair more uncomfortable, I sit. I wince as the legs wobble and creak under my weight.

Faye walks past me to sit at her desk— and as she does, her entire body ripples— *changes*— right before my eyes. The white dress she's wearing sinks into the olive of her skin, and in a shimmer of rippling light, her topmost epidermal layer seems to roll back, falling from her body like a liquid halo. When the shimmer finally fades, she is dark-skinned like me, and wearing a skin-tight body suit that disappears into a pair of jeans. A gun (looks like a Glock 22) sits securely in the body holster strapped to her frame.

She's the woman in the picture. The Captain.

My jaw drops. I've never seen *anything* like that before, which is saying a lot for a tech mogul on the bleeding edge.

No wonder she wasn't pissed about getting smudged or dirty. She *literally* just changed her skin and clothes, and maybe even her entire genetic makeup for all I knew. She did it with just a thought, just like a...

"Just like a chameleon," I whisper. "I see. The *Camille*. Right?"

"Wow. You *do* learn quickly."

"I'm sure this is the part where you explain what the hell is going on." And just as she opens her mouth, I lift my hand. "I'm not really in the mood for one of those mystical, philosophical monologues about life and death, and hard choices, and how I've been chosen to save the world or whatever. If we could get to the point quickly."

She looks at me, amused.

"Fine. Simply, we stole both your autotech and nanotechnology to set up a top secret organization of form-shifting black op agents called The Camille, whose sole purpose is to keep The Balance."

"The Balance between what?"

"Man and machine."

"Oh." I guess maybe I *should* have let her warm me up with all that philosophical crap. "I see." A long pause. Faye just looks at me, smirking. "How did—"

"We found you because your AI steward, Dan, saw the Bridget-46 model leave your residence without you. He called your phone and didn't get a response, so he put in a op request to one of our agents."

I blinked. "Op request. Like black ops assassins, or something?"

"Only when we have to be. We kill only when not doing so would affect The Balance. But that's a small part of our jobs here. We run all different kinds of operations that have nothing to do with violence. Investigation. Surveillance. Social work, counseling, and therapy. Retrieval and replacement. Traffic stops. Rehabilitation and release. The latter is the program you're in now."

"Rehab and release."

"Yes."

"Well... that's *great!*" My excitement spills out of me as I sit up straight in my chair. Guess I was going to get out of here and to my private island sooner than I thought. "Sooo, when do I get released, then?"

Faye purses her lips, and that's when I get it: there will be no release. "I am sorry," she says. "The extent of the damage done to your body was significant. We expect a rather speedy recovery now that you are awake and mobile, but not for another few weeks, at least." She looks at me. There's more. "In the meantime, we are hoping to win you over."

"Win me over... for *what*?"

"Permanent tenure. As a Camille."

I blink. "You're joking, right? Haha-I'm-on-candid-camera kind of joking, right?"

"I do not jest, Mrs. Ramoni. With all due respect to your recent losses, with what we know is coming, you are an asset to our organization. We could use your spunk. And your tech brilliance."

I ignore the compliments to get to the real tea. "What, exactly, is coming?"

"This is the part where I give you that 'mystical, philosophical monologue about life, death, and hard choices, and how you've been chosen to save the world' lecture you asked me *not* to give."

Ooooohhh nooooooo...

I immediately stand up and raise my hands, already washing them of the mess Faye was trying to put in them. "Listen. I'm super grateful for all of your wonderful help. I'm really happy to be alive and all. Truly. But saving the world, or whatever? *Not* on the agenda."

"Mrs. Ramoni—"

"No. I literally just got my entire life ripped to shit, and now that I have some modicum of it back, you want me to do, what? Save the world from whatever dumb danger it's in? No. Not gonna happen. Women like me? Divorcees with nothing left? We don't go on epic hero quests. We go on trips to Aruba to get shitfaced and titty-fucked by the local beefcakes twenty years our junior so we don't feel like we've failed as women. We drink cheap wine. We go shoe shopping. We get full body makeovers with Black Sea mud and artisanal kelp, or whatever, that we can't afford. And then, maybe once we've cleaned ourselves up a bit, we return to society, ready to share our shattered self-esteem and "life lessons" with all the other divorced PTA moms who caught their husbands banging the secretary. *That's* the life I want to live."

"It's a sad life. Especially for someone as accomplished as you."

"Sure, but it's the one I now have left, and I'll be damned if I'm not going to live it."

"But this is where your logic fails, Mrs. Ramoni. As I've been intimating, you will have *no* life to live if you do not help us."

"Maybe it would have been better to seek my help *before* stealing my tech to put together your little Charlie's Angels club. Or even *before* I had my entire company snatched away from me. Or, even *before* me and my husband were murdered—"

"You mean before you murdered your husband."

My words jam in my throat, and all my thoughts come to a screeching halt. Not sure if she said what I *thought* she said, I narrow my eyes. "Excuse me?"

"You said that your husband was murdered. You used passive voice, as though his death occurred in the most intransitive sense. As though you had nothing to do with it."

"I didn't."

"On the contrary. You *did*."

Faye pulls out a drawer on her side of the desk, and in the next moment, an old newspaper is flopping down in front of me. I don't even have to open the pages because right before my eyes, on the front page, is a detailed documentation of my last moments of life:

TECH MOGUL & EX-HUSBAND DEAD IN APPARENT MURDER-SUICIDE.

I gloss over the details, all set in small black letters.

In a shocking development, the bodies of tech mogul Andrea Rachel Ramoni, and her estranged husband David Ramoni, found in bathroom of mansion. Detectives rule crime an apparent murder-suicide. Pleasure-AUT, philanthropist, and newly-minted wife of David Ramoni, Bridget Ramoni, in shock.

Another newspaper flops down on top of the one I'm reading, dated only a week later.

Coroner concludes David Ramoni suffered torture at the hands of his estranged wife, Drea Ramoni, via an administration of a virulent nanite infection. "The muscles in his face had been completely eaten away by the infection," said Dr. Greg Meier of Alacra Medical. "Once they got into his brain

stem, he unfortunately didn't stand a chance. He would have experienced about twenty minutes of agony before he died."

Another newspaper flops down, this one more recent.

Defective nanites that caused deadly nanite infection, now called The Scourge, traced back to DefTek satellite lab in the Arctic.

My eyes widen, and on impulse, I look up and grab the next two articles out of Faye's hands.

DefTek stock plummets in the wake of criminal investigation over The Scourge.

But it's the last article that seals the deal for me. It shows the perfectly-polished face of the bitch who set me up. She stands solemnly at the press podium of a company. *My* company.

On the brink of a well-publicized sale, Bridget Ramoni steps into DefTek leadership as CEO, looking to rebrand

and restore the public's trust in the autotech industry.

There it all is. My legacy and life's work is forever stamped in ink, and it's a lie. My eyes snap up to Faye. She sits there, looking at me, grave and silent. Still, the raging fire I feel in my gut must show in my face, because her eyes are alight with triumph. She has my full attention, and she knows it.

"So," she begins. I can see a touch of a smirk in her face. "What was that you were saying about not giving a shit?"

NINE

THE SAG

FAYE CAN BARELY LEAD the tour she's taking me on, because I'm mad, ready to kick ass, and I'm rushing her through it. She leads me through the never-ending warehouse, which stretches for a mile or two both above ground and under it. The entire set up blurs under my rage: medical facilities, combat training facilities, education programs, a bunch of human and autotech workers that I couldn't give a shit about, yeah, yeah, whatever—

"Where are the bombs?" I ask finally.

Faye looks at me, wide-eyed. "What?"

"The bombs. Preferably something military-grade. The ones that can level an entire tech complex, to be more specific."

Faye blinks. "Mrs. Ramoni. I'm afraid we have no such technology. And even if we did, I'd be reluctant to let you anywhere near it in your current state."

"In my current state, you'd be a fool not to!" I roar.

As I try to blow past her, she slides smoothly in front of me. She's a lot faster than I give her credit for.

"I understand your ire. You've been set up, and your

name and life's work is being dragged through the mud," she says. "And while that is unfortunate for you and your plans to, in your words, allow men to copulate with your mammary glands, it has given us a distinct advantage in the fight to come. It has given us you. And as a valuable resource, we don't want to waste you by rushing you through our orientation process."

"I'm not interested in a fucking orientation process!" I snarl. "And I'm definitely not interested in being used for whatever dumb cause you saved me for. All I want is Bridget's head on a fucking pike."

Whup that trick! Whup that trick!

The nanites that are now a part of me have finally joined in on my mental firestorm. This time, I don't try to quiet them. I try to walk past her again, and she blocks me. Again.

"And if you work with us, you *will* get that," she says. "But if you do anything else, you won't get very far, I promise you." She looks at something, or someone, behind me and raises her hand.

By the darkness I suddenly feel on my back, I swear she'd summoned Satan himself. Fists clenched, I whip around, coming face-to-face with another woman. This one looks far less excited to see me and far less patient. A sharp green gaze cuts across my face from beneath the bangs of a pastel pink pixie cut, and though her hands are jammed into the pockets of her jeans, I get the impression that they've killed before.

I turn to her full-on, just in case she plans on adding another body to her count.

"Roi, this is Ramoni," Faye says.

"Big whoop," she mutters.

"Ramoni, this is Roi."

"Who cares," I snap back.

"Well!" Faye smiles and claps her hands together. "Glad we're all on the same page!" She turns to me. "Roi will be taking you to the acclimation facility to complete your rehabilitation. Then she'll bring you back, and we'll continue the orientation."

When I shoot Faye an annoyed look, she only claps me on the shoulder gently. "Trust me," she says. "By the time you get there, you'll be glad you went. Now get moving." She nods at Roi before she walks off. "Bring her back in one piece, Roi. Please and thank you."

As she calls this over her shoulder I start to wonder who is the bigger jerk here: me or Roi. Roi glares at me like I just killed her cat. Then she walks off, motioning for me to follow her.

Guess I'm going to find out.

CLEARLY THIS MUST BE some kind of joke.

When we arrive at the acclimation facility, I step out of the car and look up. And up. And up some more. The "facility" is actually just a huge crappy tank; the kind you could imagine a baby giant scrubbing his back in. It had to be over half a mile high and half as wide. Tall, dark steel reinforces its sides; I can't see inside it, but I can hear liquid sloshing against its walls.

I frown. Gross.

Honestly, I wasn't expecting the Marriott, but we'd just walked through an entire mile-long laboratory that looked like a royal aquarium. I'd seen sleek convalescent pods, water therapy stations, marine life study pools, and even an mollusc tank, where they'd captured and housed a *real*

Octopod. A state-of-the-art Sri Lankan technology that I'd been dying to get my hands on for years. I'd had some sexy ideas for octopoidal nanotech integration, but their patents had been impenetrable. And somehow, The Camille just *had* one. Out of nowhere. They had *all* this in general— literally millions of dollars in lab technology— just sitting here.

So now that I see that I'm getting the shittiest tank in the whole lab, I glare at Roi.

"Seriously? What is this?" These are my first words to her in our entire thirty-minute journey.

"This is the only way you get to walk away from this." She responds. And when I look at her as though she's lost her mind, she smiles and indicates the right side of my body with her chin. "Literally."

That's when I feel it– the unmistakable pull of gravity on the side of my body that Bridget has completely destroyed. My face, even the skin on my skull, begin to sag downward. I try to lift my hand to stop it, to hold it in place, but I find that my muscles are slow to respond. Heavy neural damage has taken hold again, degrading my response time to only a fraction of what it was. The temporary transmitters the doctors put into my body seem to be sparking out, now unable to create chemical bridges between my brain and the muscles I seek to control. At once, an entire side of my body crumples, and it's a struggle to even remain standing.

Roi seems to be enjoying every single minute of it.

"Wasss aaappening to me—" Only the left side of my face can ask this question, but I gave Roi all of the anger I can out of my half glare and semi-frown.

"The same thing that happens to all you rich jerks when

you stop shoving botox up your asses. You're starting to sag, sweetie. Gravity's a bitch, ain't it?"

"I neber gotten work done o' me in my entire sthucking lifthe," I snarl, the enraged slurring against the muscles that won't respond. "Buhlack don't crack, *sthweetie.*"

Roi cut me a look that's only half convinced. She pulls a three prong syringe from her back pocket and plunges it into my sagging thigh. The pain is sharp, but quick, and before she pulls the syringe away I can already feel my skin, muscles, and joints tightening back up. As my lips and chin readhere to my jawbone, I rub my face, relieved.

"Christ on a cracker," I mutter. "The hell was that?"

"Your nanites. They don't seem to like you very much."

I blink, feeling as dumb as I sound. I'd been invaded by my own tech, and I hadn't even realized it. I'd panicked, much as David did with his own infection. Still, I threw Roi a pissed look. "You guys knew The Scourge was coming for me, and you didn't even tell me?"

"Oh, were we supposed to brief you while your brains were spread out on a stretcher?"

I open my mouth to respond, but she has a point. So I bite down. Roi walks towards the tank, and I follow her.

"The nanites need to acclimate to the body they're in," Roi continues. "Or they will literally turn on it. Like—"

"Like an immune system that doesn't recognize its own cells," I mutter bitterly. "Yeah, I get it."

"Heh. Not such an idiot after all." She hits a button on the side of the tank, and spiral stairs materialize from the metal.

"Why would I be?" I snap back. "I *built* the prototype of that ecosystem, remember?"

"Whatever. *You* say you're Drea Ramoni. *I* say you haven't proven it yet. Here's your chance."

I stand in front of the stairs that will take me at least ten minutes to climb. More even, because I'm still on the mend.

"The serum I shot into your leg is a temporary solution," Roi says. "Really only to calm the nanites down. You want something permanent, you get into the tank. Or the same thing that happened to David Ramoni will happen to you. Sans the revenge murder, of course."

"I *didn't* murder him."

"Yeah. Whatever part deux. You haven't proven that either. Now." Roi turns and indicates the ladder at the side of the tank. "Up you go."

It takes twice as long as I predicted to mount each stair, and the higher I climb, the colder and windier it gets. I wrap my arms around my chest as wind tears through my bomber. On some level I can feel the microripples in my blood as the nanites once again begin to stir. Either they're trying to warm me up, or they're getting ready to eat me alive again. The thought of the latter quickens my ascent.

At the top of the tank is just what I imagined. A platform runs around the tank's circumference, and inside the tank itself are thousands upon thousands of gallons of water. The blood in my veins continues to warm. I step forward and peek over the edge of the platform. I see no bottom to the tank. Just an unending darkness, a roiling void of abyss with a glacée of white sunlight on its surface.

"You don't have much time." Roi's voice comes at me from my right, tinny and spackled with static. I turn to see a small, rusting intercom jutting up from the platform's surface behind me. "You dive, or you degrade. Make your choice."

"*Where* do I swim? What direction?"

"The only direction that matters."

"For how long?"

I get no explanation to this question. Roi is done with me, and so are the nanites, apparently. I can feel them more vividly now. My body warms up, and I'm starting to feel it again: the sag.

Holding back tears, I step to the edge and take the deepest breath I can, all the while praying that this new body of mine will be strong enough to make it. I dive in, swimming down into the deep.

TEN

THE DIVE

BITTER.

That's how the water tastes as it fills my ears and nose, and yet, I continue to swim the only direction that matters: down. My strokes are paralyzed by atrophy. Worse I can't see the bottom toward which I struggle. It feels so vast, so endless...

95 feet.

My limbs haven't fully connected to the rest of me; they jerk out of my control as I try to command them. The frantic thrum of my heart beat in my ears, the burden of the carbon dioxide in my chest are both distractions to what I know lies at the bottom of the tank: salvation.

And still, I know I will not make it.

My body begins to cool, and yet the deep pushes against it, trying to force me back to the surface. My legs jut out behind me, useless. I am Bambi on ice.

80 feet.

A gelling of sinew, the tightening of skin, the resurrection of muscle. My strokes finally start to make sense, and my legs come alive. They flutter into a butterfly kick.

65 feet.

Kicks and strokes that are now stronger. I am propelled into the deep, and as darkness envelops me, swallows me, I fight against a growing pressure that crunches down on every bone in my body.

50 feet.

Now that I have more control over my movements, I pay more attention to my surroundings. Anchored into the sides of the tank are rows and rows of plasticlike molds. They look familiar.

Shells. That's what they are.

Human-shaped, impenetrable carapaces molded to the human form, derived from the groundbreaking Bubble technology recently developed in Jerusalem. They haunt the edges of my watery prison, mere empty husks of the people who used to occupy them.

At least, *most* are empty. Some, to my horror, are full. The jellied pulp of drowned, decaying bodies fill some carapaces up with blackened flesh, withering cartilege—

45 feet.

Warmth in my chest as my lungs begin to simmer. I fight to reach the nadir of the tank.

40 feet.

I fight. Lungs begin to stew. But I push. Because even in the dark, my eyes can see something at the bottom of the tank.

35 feet.

Lungs burning. I need air. Need air. Need air.

30 feet.

A sudden wave of neural chatter floods my brain as the murky shadows at the bottom of the tank begin to solidify.

15 feet.

Shadows and darkness become visible outlines.

Suddenly, I'm not thinking about air anymore. I can see bodies. Faces.

10 feet.

An *endless* sea of human expression. Some closed, some with their eyes wide open.

At five feet, my pounding heart slows. I can see clearly the faded plastic, chipped chins, and degraded temples. Plastic beauty forever preserved. There was no slow water rot. No gelatinous, bloated flesh of a drowned body.

The faces— the people— were not alive. They never had been. I was looking at a graveyard of plastic parts. Mannequins. Autotechs. Scattered synthetic humana.

Need air.

I release the tension in my limbs, ready to let the water buoy me back to the surface. And as I do, I reach with my fingers and caress the hard, unyielding round of a nearby mannequin's cheek. A silent goodbye.

Its eyes open. The painted beauty twists into an animal rage as its jaw drops and releases a shrill howl that I cannot hear, but that I can see and feel in the string of bubbles released from its throat. In the violence of its now human face.

I kick away, trying to get out of reach, but its hands shoot out and lock down around my arms. I struggle, and the effort eats up the last of the oxygen I have. My world quickly grows dark as the burn in my lungs turns to a boil, and I can't hold on, I can't *not* breathe anymore—

Somewhere in the distance, a metallic *clunk* reverberates through the water.

Suddenly, I'm being pulled sideways. I can feel the distant vacuum and the me that is rushing to fill it. The current is strong, so strong that I am torn from the hellish sea doll's grasp. It screams viciously as it reaches for me, its prize lost. My body, no longer under my control, tumbles through the water, sucked through the deep, and at the same time, I fade, succumbing to the black.

ELEVEN
MEETING THE TEAM

I AM BEING DRAGGED across the ground by my ankle. Gravel tears into my back and neck. Water spouts from my mouth and nose, and sunlight rips into my vision.

I cough up more water, struggling to breathe. Whoever's dragging me doesn't help my body to purge. They simply pull, and all I can do is try my best to pivot so that my skin and hair isn't sloughed off as they do.

After what feels like an eternity I'm thrown into a small, dry space. Warm folds are dumped onto my head and body. Towels. Blankets, maybe. Then something above me folds down and locks, casting me into complete darkness.

That sea of bodies and faces. That *thing* that tried to drown me. It'd looked completely synthetic, and then... I grip the places on my arms where it grabbed me, where bone and flesh instead of silicone had dug into my skin. What the hell *was* that?

The car starts, and I realize that, whether I want to or not, I'm probably going to find out.

THE CAR FINALLY STOPS, and after 20 minutes I realize that Roi's forgotten about me. Probably not by accident. I pivot and find the seat lock. If the gods love me, I'll be able to get into backseat area through the trunk. If not, well, I'm screwed.

I do my best to jimmy the lock in the dark. I finally get the right leverage and push— and I let out a 'woot' when sunlight filters into the trunk.

Awesome.

I push harder and the backseat opens into Roi's car. I squeeze through and tumble head first. When I right myself I see that the car's still empty, and it's parked in the lot we'd originally started in. I reach into the front seat, unlock the doors, and let myself out.

The fresh air I suck into my lungs is tinged with car oil and carbon. Aside from that, though, the warehouse lot is completely desolate. I look around for any familiarities, and I find one: the hallway that Faye had originally led me through after we'd left her office. I follow my instincts and head through. I'm pretty sure I'm halfway back to her when I hear laughter. Roi's laughter.

"Not my fault she passed out," the voice chuckled. "Figured if she wanted a nap, she could just stay in there 'til she was done."

Definitely Roi. And apparently whoever was listening to her thought she was a riot because the entire room erupted in a chorus of snickers. I continue walking forward, towards the light spilling out of a doorway, where they're all hanging out.

"Aw, that's really mean guys." A voice I don't recognize chimes in, a pitch above the rest. "We don't treat recruits that way! Faye said so herself!"

"She's not a recruit. She's a stray that got hit on the road. Faye's wasting our time on someone who didn't come to us on her own. Total waste."

This is when I round the corner and step into the room. There are about five women hanging out around a brewing coffee pot. Though I assume they are all a part of The Camille, each of them looks completely different. All different ethnicities, all dressed differently, all varying heights and weights... like there was a "diversity matters" convention going on that I hadn't heard about. None of them see me as I walk in, so the conversation continues:

"Wonder how long she'll stay in there," says one in over-alls and a bandanna.

"Not that long, apparently," I mutter dryly.

They all turn, and the overall'd one smiles and winks at me. "There you are! Lookin' good, D."

"Who the hell are you?" I ask.

"Only one of the medics who saved your ass," Roi snaps back. She'd been leaning against one of the counters but now sways to a stand. "A thank you would work just fine."

"You expect me to thank you for leaving me to suffocate in the trunk of a car? What happened to *not* killing me, like Faye said?"

Roi smirks. "She said to bring you back in one piece. Not to bring you back alive."

"Well, we'll see how Faye feels about that little interpretation of her rules."

"Oh, really? You're a snitch now? Thought you'd have a little more heart than that." Roi steps towards me, and I can see the muscles in her arms and neck flex as she does. "But I guess you really *are* just some powdered princess in need of saving."

"Without this powdered *princess*, you wouldn't even have the tech to walk and talk the way you do. So maybe it's *you* who should be thanking *me*. Not the other way around."

A chorus of "ooo"s and "oh snap"s rise up from the group of girls, some mocking and some not. Roi's cheeks flush red and she steps into my face. I don't budge.

"I could literally mop the floor with you, you—"

"Mop the floor? Oh, you're the domestic type. Figures. You've got the smarts for it."

Roi's fist cocks back, but before it can make contact, another Camille grabs her wrist and shirt collar from behind and yanks her. Its the one in the overalls and bandanna. She chuckles as she pulls Roi away and shoves her into a chair. Roi huffs and folds her arms, seeming to submit to the woman's authority.

"Better listen to her, Roi," she said. "I put her in a coma seven times. Stubborn bitch refused to stay down." The overall'd chick then looks at me, and I realize the smirk on her face is admiration, not resentment. "Guess that's a recurring theme." She sticks out her hand. "I'm Tren."

Remembering my quiet promise to be nice, I take Tren's hand and shake it. "Drea."

"Faye's not here. She and her crew went into the city for a supply run. She told us to take you through phase three until she gets back."

"Was that why I got locked in a car trunk?" I cut Roi a poisonous look. She smirks back, finally landing the blow she wanted.

"Nah, that was just Roi introducing herself. Phase Three is to help you get those 'voices' of yours under control. Chica?"

On "chica", Tren turns around to address a Camille that I haven't seen yet. It's because she's shrunk herself down into a corner behind one of the counters. Now she creeps up over the edge shyly to peek out at me. I blink, shocked. Pigtails, freckles, spectacles all compliment a thin frame in a T-shirt, ripped jeans, and high-top sneakers. As she stands to her full height (which is only about four and a half feet), I can see the comics and books she carries under her arm. The girl couldn't have been any older than twelve or thirteen.

Chica looks at me, adjusts her glasses, and smiles sheepishly. "Hi!"

"Take Drea to Phase 3. You'll be attending to her."

"Ooh, exciting!" She skips around the counter, pushes past the rest of the Camille, and reaches for my hand. Unsure of what else to do, I take it.

"Come on!" She chirps. "Follow me!"

I don't have much of a choice, really, but the girl's enthusiasm somehow cuts through my suspicion and makes me feel better. I allow her to pull me along.

"Good luck, Drea," Tren says. "This is the last easy thing you'll get to do."

The last *easy* thing?

I shoot a final look over my shoulder and notice the now grave faces of everyone in the room. No more laughs, no more games, no more jeers. She's dead serious, and I am afraid for what her words mean. The murder of my ex-husband, getting shot in the head, dying, coming back to life. Being framed, finding out my entire life's work is being used as a jizz tissue. Swimming through a chemical tank with decaying limbs, nearly getting drowned by a zombie doll, and then left in the locked trunk of a car... none of these things *felt* easy at all. I'm not sure if I'm ready for things to get harder.

But Chica is already dragging me into Phase Three. So whether I'm ready for this or not, it's obvious I don't have much of a choice.

TWELVE

THE CREW

WE'RE IN A DRIVERLESS CAR. This one's name is Korinne. She's nice enough, but I really miss Dan, and it's the first time he's crossed my mind since all this crazy shit's happened.

Chica decides to take front passenger seat, and she convinces me to sit in the back. I don't argue, especially since this means I can lay down and relax for once. I'm tired as hell, and it's nice to ride on the actual inside of a car, rather than in a trunk.

I ask where we're going, and I get the response I expected: the ole cryptic "you'll see!". Oh, brother. Why everything has to be so mysterious is beyond me, but from what Chica's telling me, this is the most exciting thing to happen to her in a long time. She gets to take me into Phase 3... and it's her *first* Phase 3 trainee *ever*.

"I wasn't old enough before," she explains. "But I am now, and I'm AMPED! This is *so* exciting, don't you think?"

"Sure, kid. Real exciting." I'm not really listening, but I let out a long, happy sigh as I sink into the buttery velvet of the backseat. The steady hum of the engine is all I feel, and it relaxes me, massaging my bones. Goddamn, this is comfortable.

"You look so cozy and snug!"Chica says. She smiles as she looks at me over her headrest. "Which is great, because you'll need to be super comfortable for this part."

Wait, what? I start to sit up. "What part are you—"

A thick metal sheet slams closed between me and the front seat, separating me from Chica. Alarmed, I shoot up and try both door handles. Then I rear back and kick the metal sheet. No luck. I'm totally locked in.

"HEY!" I scream and kick the sheet again. "WHAT THE HELL, KID?!"

"Don't worry, Mrs. Ramoni. You're perfectly safe. It's just that they can't really focus with outside distractions."

"Who's *they*?"

"Your crew."

"My... what?"

"The nanites we installed in your brain that are, you know, keeping you alive? That's what we call them: your crew." Her voice reverberates through the metal. "We're on our way to the training facility, but you both need to acclimate to each other. In a comfortable, safe space."

"I thought the acclimation tank was supposed to take care of that."

"That only put them to sleep. So they and your body wouldn't try to fight each other off. But, like, they have feelings too, you know? So you have to make nice with them. Talk to them, love them. It's like an arranged marriage or whatever. Neither of you really know each other, but you'll be together forever, so you'll have to make due, sort of thing."

"What? But that doesn't even make any—"

"OH!" Chica squeals suddenly. "I've got something for you, too! Tren said you'd probably want a drink?"

A drink. Huh. Well, guess this wasn't going to be so bad after all.

"TADAAAA!!!"

My "drink" pops up from the middle arm rest. But instead of a dirty martini, all I see is a milkshake. With cookies in it. And a pink bendy straw. I scowl.

"A fucking *milk*shake, kid? You've gotta be kidding me."

"Not a milkshake, Mrs. Ramoni. A *malt* shake. Big difference! Anyways, hope you like it, and good luck! We'll be at the facility soon!"

I grumble, but I snatch the malt shake from the cup holder and sip. Huh. It *was* pretty good—

Good in the hood, and if we could, then we would, and—

I sigh and roll my eyes. They were back. Here we go... "Ok, guys." I sigh. I take another sip. "So, we didn't get off to the greatest start with the whole 'let's tear off your face' thing, and I totally get it. No hard feelings. So maybe we can start over?"

"Start over the Rover's, the stove or the clover—"

"Without the dumb lyrics, please?! Honestly, what's with that?"

Silence.

I run my hands through my braids, trying to calm down. "Okay. Sorry. I was a little harsh. Maybe we'll do something a little easier, like make small talk, so that we can all just—"

"How about you *do something easier, like fucking your mother?"*

Holy crap. That was a strong reaction. I grit my teeth, trying to stay calm. "Well you know what, guys? Maybe I don't want to go bang my mother. Maybe, despite the fact that I didn't have one, I still think it's important to *respect* mothers," I snap. "She gave me life, after all."

"We gave you life!" The crew snaps back. Silently, of course. I can't hear them, but for whatever reason, I know what they're saying.

"Okay. You're right. Thanks for that. But still, so... what? What do *you* want to do, then? Be at each other's throats every minute? Or do you want to survive?"

"Of course we want to survive! But what the hell's the point in talking to you? This 'relationship' isn't going to work out anyway."

"I don't know. Maybe since we'll be sharing the same mind for, well, pretty much the rest of our lives, we should try to make it work."

"They bounce me from one body to another, and it never works out. None of my hosts last long enough."

"What, do you give them brain tumors or something? Walk them off cliffs?"

"No. We just don't get along so great."

"Well, have you considered that maybe you're kind of a dick?"

"No, but if you keep insulting me, I'll make sure you wake up with one. Asshole."

"Yeah, whatev— wait." I sit up, creasing my brow. "You can do that? Like, turn me into a man?"

"With a bit of practice, and the right biological components, I can turn you into nearly anything. That's why you're called a Camille. Haven't you been paying attention?"

"Yes, but... wait. Did you just call *me* a Camille?"

I can both hear and feel the nanites' dark chuckles in my flesh. *"Yeah. That's the fine print on this whole charity thing Faye's got going on. It's one thing to be extracted, or retrieved and replaced. But rehab and release? Getting raised from the dead? That's a whole different type of tamale, baby. If you get rebuilt with their tech, then you become theirs. Did you really think they were gonna just patch you up and let you walk out of here with me?"*

Actually, I did. I had never considered for one moment that I was a prisoner. Faye had never quite put it that way.

"She never does." My crew says, reading my thoughts. *"And she never will. She will let you walk out of here, sure. But as soon as you turn to leave, she'll put a bullet in your head. And this time, she won't bring you back. Don't believe me? Next time you get a chance, ask those stiffs at the bottom of the acclimation tank."*

My eyes widen. Just as I'm about to open my mouth, I remember that Chica is in the front seat, Listening. So instead, I force a thought through my mind: *Why are you telling me this?*

"Because this is my last chance... and I don't want to die." This is the first time I feel emotion from them. Fear. *"Do you?"*

"No," I say softly. "I don't want to die."

We share a silence, and in my gut I know we've reached an agreement.

"Okay then," I think. *"Let's keep it real simple. We work together, and we live. I won't leave you if you won't leave me. Okay?"*

The collective *hurrumph* I feel in my body is precisely the type of submission I'm looking for. Mutual survival. The peacekeeper of all peacekeepers. It's not a perfect truce, but it'll do.

I smile, feeling triumphant for the first time since getting here. Daylight warms my face as the heavy metal on the windows finally begins to recede into the door. *"One last thing. I'm not anyone's prisoner. The Camille are cool, and I am grateful to you all for what you've done for me. But I don't plan on sticking around for long."*

"Yeah, that's what they all say... until they see it."

I feel my brows knit together, reflexively. "See what?"

My "crew" lifts my chin, using it to point at one of the car windows. "See *that*."

I follow their direction, and I squint, hard. Because what I'm seeing looks completely unreal. Impossible.

It doesn't take me long to decide that looking at it through the glass won't be good enough. I roll down the window and stick my head through, unable to take my eyes off it.

A city. Looming, vast... and *living*.

Its horizon morphs and changes right before my eyes as skyscrapers disintegrate into sand on a whim. Shorter buildings increase their height in tandem, reaching for the heavens. Even the roads manage to erase and rebuild themselves, seeming to disappear in some places while forming pathways and alleys through others.

"Wow. It's... changing?" I whisper. "All the time?"

"All the time," my crew says. *"A city designed almost completely on and of nanotech. Our city. And it's a city you helped build."*

THIRTEEN

THE CHANGING CITY

I WALK the streets of the changing city, looking at everything and yet nothing, because nothing stays there long enough to be looked at. We'd parked on a side street by a meter, and by the time we got out of the car, the parking meter had already been replaced by an old bagel cart. No bagel *guy*, though. Just a cart.

Still. That was nothing compared to how the empty lot behind the cart suddenly spun up into a jazz club. Again, with no patrons, bouncers, or workers. But the neon lights and broken musical notes floating through the open door give an impression of a forgotten nightlife, now withering on the vine.

"Does anyone live here?" I ask.

"Yup!" Chica twitters. She seems completely unfazed by the chaos. "But they're pretty nomadic and unpredictable. You kinda have to be in order to survive here."

"Yeah…" I murmur as I watch a little pizza shop reform. Then, either the nanites get bored or the wind blasts too hard, because the top of the pizza shop suddenly scatters away in the wind, like a film of dust being blown from an old counter. The nanites leave an open-roofed pizza patio in their wake. Which would look kind of cool as a dating spot... except no one is sitting there.

"How is this possible?"

"Trillions and trillions and trillions of gazillions of AI nanites, drawing on organic and inorganic matter in the environment. Minerals, elements, human cells, animal cells... the nanites bond with all of them. They mimic, reanimate, and rebuild the composition of most things they attach to. Sometimes with necessary and added upgrades. But this—" Chica motions around, indicating the entire city. "Is the result of when autotech, nanotech, and inorganic and organic matter shed their cells into the environment and find each other."

"But how do the nanites know to work together and use these things to build entire cities?"

"Because we programmed them that way!" She smiles at me. "But as you can see, the nanites are... a little confused nowadays."

Yeah, tell me about it.

That they were "confused" was an understatement. The city couldn't decide what it wanted to be, and when the nanites *did* make a decision to become a series of buildings, or parking garages, or even something as simple as a village bazaar with kiosks, they seemed unable to make themselves look nice.

In fact? Everything the city chooses to be is total trash.

Even the buildings that pass the five-minute longevity test don't look welcoming in the least. All that line the streets are dilapidated businesses, charred lofts, and a few condemned buildings— one of which me and Chica are walking by just now.

This building in particular looks hella creepy. It's not

very tall, but it towers over me nonetheless. The windows are blown out. The glass that was in them is scattered across the sidewalk. At least I *assume* so, because it's so dark within that I can't see very much. The door is boarded up, and nailed to it is a ragged sign with large, spray-painted letters that read: CONDEMNED.

A whisper of the past as I remember what it was like to live in one of these as a child. A life I lived before I found the library bathroom and made it my home. I shudder, and I keep walking, wanting to get away from it as quickly as possible. I don't notice that Chica's not following me until I hear her shout from behind.

"Hey, blind-y, it's right here! Phase 3!"

I whip around to see her standing in front of the run-down building, waving her arms at me. No freaking way. Please, please do *not* tell me that this is where Phase 3 is. As I walk back up to her, she motions to go through the decrepit, boarded doors. I hang my head.

Crap. It is.

I close my eyes and take a breath before I dare to look back up at the shit hole I'm about to step into— and when I open them again, I am shocked to see that what was a rat-infested garbage heap is now literally brand-spanking-new. I take a step back, eyes wide.

The crumbling ledges above me are gone, now replaced with a colorful awning. The singed brick is now bright and clean. I look at Chica, shocked, and when I turn back to the building, I see that the blown-out windows have widened and grown in height. All the broken glass is gone, replaced with crystal clear panes, through which a soft, warm light emanates. Some of the glass panes even have drawings on them.

Doodles of candies. Pastries. Lots of ice cream cones.

The glass sports a business name, which is spackled onto the storefront in a hyper-feminine, curlicue font: The Camille Confectionery.

I look at Chica blankly. A candy store. We are going shopping at a freaking candy store. *This* is Phase 3.

FOURTEEN

THE CONFECTIONERY

"WELCOME TO PHASE THREE!" Chica giggles. She makes her announcement with an unusual amount of flair and flings open the doors of the confectionery dramatically.

"This is Phase Three?" I mutter.

"Yes!" She claps her hands together. "I designed it myself, just for you! The confectionery of doooom..." As she says "dooom", she makes a face and wiggles her fingers as though she's some sort of ghoul.

I raise my eyebrows as I look over "the confectionary of doom", which actually just looks like a really lovely ice cream and candy parlor. I frown.

"Well, what are you waiting for? Let's go train!"

"But what— how is this 'Phase 3'?"

"Well, you're not gonna find out by just standing around, are ya? Ooh, I just can't *wait!*" She squeals and runs in front of me, disappearing into the rainbow-colored bowels of the shop. Having little choice, I follow her in.

As soon as I step over the threshold, the doors automatically swing closed behind me. The light airy tinkle of the door chimes and the roaring nanite traffic are the last sounds I hear before we're sealed away from the world outside.

With just one look around, I immediately understand why Chica dragged me here. I'm not a kid, but goddamn... this was a sweet tooth heaven that not even *I* could have designed.

Bright pastels and soft candy colors splash the walls, from floor to ceiling. On the left, a sugarglass ice cream freezer runs across the entire length of the store. On the right hang candies, sweets, chocolates, and confections of every single kind. Cotton candy, taffy, and flavored popcorn machines stand vigils in each corner and everything in here gives off a sweet, seductive smell. Sickening, really. But seductive. At the front of the shop hang big colorful tote bags, with the words "FILL ME" embroidered onto them.

"Get thee behind me, Satan," I mutter. Fuck the Paleo diet; I was ready to fill my own shopping bag like there was no tomorrow.

Further into the shop, Chica no longer pays me any mind. She checks her own list and compares confections like she's making life decisions.

I crease my brow and look around. "Where's the store owner?"

"We *are* the store owners."

"How do people pay if no one is manning the counter?"

Chica looks up and smiles. She looks thrilled to be able to teach me something. "They don't. No one knows this is here. This is for Phase 3 training only."

"But *how* does this count as training?"

"Try to pick out something to eat, and you'll see. Go ahead," she says. She looks back down at her list as she does. "Make a choice! It's all real, fresh, and it's all on us!" She continues her shopping.

I smirk as I watch her flit from wall to wall. "Okay, kid," I say. "Since you're Miss Money Bags all of a sudden, why not?"

I travel the length of the ice cream freezer and gaze through the glass to see literally every single flavor ice cream known to man: vanilla, french-vanilla, chocolate, fudge chocolate, chocolate-chocolate, chunky monkey, cookies and cream, candy and cream, butterscotch, coffee. Dozens of flavors. They go on and on, but they're nothing compared to what's sitting on the counter above them.

Waffle cones, sugar cones, belgian waffle cones, waffle bowls, crepes, candy cups. Fudge, brownies, peanut brittle, devil's food cake, angel's food cake, undecided food cake, mille crepe cake, cupcakes...

Nougats.

Pastries.

Pain au chocolat.

My stomach growls, and I realize that I haven't eaten at all since I've been awake. I'm starving, actually. Guess now I know why. I can feel my mouth begin to water as I start to think about what I want.

"Huh," I mutter. "What *do* I want?"

Pricks of neural activity run across the lobes of my brain. Then, the tickles turn into chatter. Chatter becomes static. When the static suddenly increases into a monstrous roar, I shriek and cover my ears. But it's not helping. Whatever this sudden interference is, it's coming from *inside* my head.

I grit my teeth as the roar crescendoes. "GOD, WHAT *IS* THAT?!"

Suddenly Chica is in front of me, shoving her shopping list into my face. Except she's turned it to the back, where she's written huge letters: IT'S YOUR CREW. MAKE

THEM CHOOSE. I shake my head and fall to one knee, almost collapsing beneath the heavy surge of sound.

Shutupshutupshutupshutup— SHUT THE HELL UP!!

I scream this in my mind, and while they slow down a bit, they don't shut up at all. I focus as hard as I can, trying to identify at least *one* voice in the crowd. I can finally pinpont a few hundred, who happen to be one of thousands clustered around my eardrums. They are shouting in unison, like a pack of psycho, sugar-high kids: *Banana cream! Chunky monkey! Laffy taffy! Banana cream! Chunky monkey! Laffy taffy!* They repeat their request over and over and over, forming a unanimous, voiceless chant that refuses to let up.

"OKAY, OKAY!" I say loudly. Chica covers her ears, and because my crew's so loud, it's the only indication I get that *I'm* now screaming too. "WE'LL GET BANANA CREAM AND CHUNKY MONKEY, *FUCK!*"

AND LAFFYTAFFY LAFFYTAFFY LAFFYLAFFY TAFFYTAFFY—

"OKAY! JESUS CHRIST, JUST SHUT THE FUCK UP!"

The undulating roar in my mind suddenly subsides, and I slump down to the floor, relieved. A second later, there's a collective moan about three billion strong. Softer this time, though. Apparently, none of the others wanted that flavor, and frankly, neither did I. I find bananas totally gross. But if it was going to keep my crew from tearing my body apart, then I was ready to eat all the bananas on the freaking planet.

Chica bounds up to me, with a bag full of all sorts of sweets. Cakes, candies, ice cream, laffy taffy. All banana flavored. Ugh. Gross.

"Looks good, kiddo," I say. I'm exhausted, but somehow

I pick myself up off the floor. "Let's grab it, and get the hell out of here."

"Yeah, wow! That was super quick. Usually newbies are in here for at least thirty minutes, writhing and suffering and— well, you know..."

Her chatter is a lot easier to ignore now that I've been aurally bulldozed by a few billion child-like candy freaks. My ears are still ringing, my head is still spinning, and my blood is churning from the heightened nanite activity. Still, somehow I'm able to stand on both feet. I lean tiredly against the counter, watching Chica's lips move as she takes out a credit scanner and swipes it across the check out machine.

The scanner beeps, and the door chime tinkles. I can't hear these things, but I can see the green light pop on as Chica's credit is accepted... and I can feel a wind on my back as the front door opens. I pay it no mind.

Not until I see Chica's jaw drop in a scream.

The first bullet tears across the round of my shoulder. I spin around as much from surprise as from the force, and that's when the second, third, and fourth bullets blast through my chest.

FIFTEEN

UPGRADED

PRESSURE FILLS the air as it splits with metal and heat.

Four explosions detonate in my back, breaking bones and splitting muscle inside. I slam into the corner of the ice cream freezer and flip over it, hitting the floor behind. The pain is so great, so all-consuming, that I almost can't even feel it. While I can't hear anything else, I can *feel* something shrill and terrified reverberate through my body. Chica's screams. She's calling me, calling my name—

"Ch-chica—?" I inhale, and I get nothing but a mouth and chest full of blood. I cough, spraying crimson across the floor, across the rusty bottom of the ice cream freezer. On reflex, tears fill my eyes. I can't feel anything in my limbs, just heavy bits of flesh, devoid of life.

I'm dying, and I'm going a lot more slowly than the first time. I can feel the thunder of boots hitting the ground, the soft rustle of cloth, air parting for bodies moving through space— another of Chica's screams tears through me. Whoever it is, they've got her. They've got her, and there's nothing I can—

A jolt flashes through my temples, and something deep

inside my gut seems to click. In my chest I can feel something, some*things* closing flesh, sewing up muscle, purging blood.

What...? What's happening?

"Breathe." A voice I recognize. My crew.

I breathe, and this time, I can actually taste something other than blood. Oxygen. I take another breath, deep. I can feel parts of my body again, and with the low hum I can feel under my skin, I can tell my crew is working hard to rebuild themselves. To rebuild *me*. The pain hasn't receded, but I try to sit up anyway, because the door chime is tinkling, and Chica's screams are getting farther away. I try to rise, and I manage to slump against the opposite wall. I've got to get up, got to—

A shadow spills over me as someone tall and broad rounds the corner of the ice cream freezer.

"Bitch is still breathin'..." he mutters. I see him walk towards me, and as he does, he lifts a shotgun. "I'll fix that right quick."

Guys, we're about to get wasted, better think of something quick.

"*Do we have to do* everything?!" My crew snaps back at me.

My right hand suddenly heats up, and it clenches down into a fist, hard. My fist tightens harder. Harder still until it hurts, until my bones are literally bending, breaking.

I have no idea what the hell is going on with my body, and I don't dare look down because this guy is coming for me. As he advances, I try to take him in, see who he is.

A twisted half-mouth. Squished, troll like nose. Dark, menacing eyes, one of which has a split lid. His face looks like his mom shat it out on her way to work, but more importantly, it's a face I recognize.

I know him. He was in one of those mugshots in Faye's office.

He's on me now, and as he gets closer, this time for a headshot, he cocks the shottie and smiles. Instinctively, I lift my arms to shield my head, and as I do, he stops in his tracks. As he looks at me, at my *arm*, his eyes widen. And for that matter, so do mine. Because neither of us can believe what were seeing.

"What the fuck?" Terrified, he takes a step back.

My arm is a mangled skeletal mess. Its flesh peels back, exposing glistening bone, which then begins to break. From knuckles to wrist, my arm cracks, changes, recedes, and transforms, and at the same time, I feel my rage divert from gut to wrist, converting to something hot and dangerous. My rolled back flesh hardens into something strong, thick. *Metallic*. Without my crew even telling me, I finally know what's going on. As does my attacker, apparently, as I lift my arm and *aim* it at him.

Aim.

Because holyfuckingshit. My arm is a fucking CANNON.

The guy takes another step back, and I am no longer afraid. I smirk, close one eye, steady my aim. I have no idea who this fucker is, but he's about to have a really bad day.

"OH SH—"

Whatever he's about to say gets lost in the heat and light of the particle beam from my cannon. The middle of his body disintegrates, and as it does the pieces that are left of him slam into the far wall, spattering on impact.

Before his ashes and charred parts crumble to the ground, I'm already blowing open the doors of the Confectionery. I walk through, like a BOSS. A muscle car idles in front, and one of the thugs is trying to shove a screaming

Chica into its trunk. I take aim at the front just as the driver spots me.

He barely gets a shot off before the cannon beam takes off his head, along with the entire front windshield. The other thug drops Chica and starts firing at me, and two more of his crew come from the other side of the car, joining in. Their bullets melt under the heat of my blasts, and so do they.

By the time I'm done, the getaway car looks like swiss cheese. That a mouse threw up. I've wrecked half a city block too. The other half, apparently, had disintegrated and fled for its own protection. As raggedy as the city's nanites are, they still had a bit of common sense, I guess. The only thing that still stands is the Confectionery, which has again taken on the appearance of an abandoned building. Except now, its boarded up doors are missing. In the doors' place is a gaping black maw, leading into decrepit darkness.

The rest of the block is completely leveled.

My body moves with a military precision that is not mine. I find Chica, who'd taken refuge under the back wheels of the car like a frightened kitten. I stand her up, brush her off, and wipe her tears before turning to search the wreckage and what's left of the bodies. I grab what I can find: a few handguns that survived, the license plate of the vehicle, some identifying information out of the jeans of a thug I just vaporized. Said thug no longer has a torso, but the bottom half of his body lays twitching on the concrete. Somehow, I don't vomit as I search him. One of the guns I shove deep into the belt of my jeans. Just in case.

I grab my candy bag from the sidewalk and dump all my findings into it. Parts of dead assholes mixed in with banana cream. Felt about right.

"In case you were wondering," my crew speaks. Their

collective voice is like the last whisper of a lullaby. *"The name's Mildred."*

Then, they power down to sleep, leaving me, Drea, in its place to take on my body's fatigue. The burden is heavy. Exhausted, I stagger, only vaguely feeling my arm power down and return to normal. Chica walks up to me, her face awash with shock. In one hand, she carries her own haul of candy and treats, salvaged from the sidewalk. She laces her fingers with mine and stands next to me, staring out into the street. We look like two trick-or-treaters who'd just gotten the crap kicked out of them. Or something.

"Thank you," she whispers.

I nod. We stand there, hand-in-hand, holding our bags of candy. We are up to our ankles in debris and ash, and yet we say nothing until Faye pulls up in her car.

THE BOTTOM HALF of the thug's body quivers in the trunk of Faye's car, and I'm pretty sure I'm the only one wondering if it's going to shit itself or something.

Faye and Chica don't seem concerned. Aside from Chica's happy humming, no words are spoken.

Faye drives, a solemn look on her face. Chica is clearly enjoying her sweets and comics in the back seat, and is listening to her headphones. Whatever trauma she endured seems to have been cleanly tucked away into the back of her mind. Good for her. Because as for me? My nerves are fucking *shot*.

I sit in the front passenger seat, and I gaze out at the long red road in front of us, trying to get myself together. I still feel a warm sting in my fingertips, palm, and wrist... all of which had changed before my very eyes into a weapon of destruction. I lift my burning hand and stare at it in awe.

Wow.

My crew was a bunch of assholes, but man, did they care about staying alive.

Still, I have more questions than ever now, and aside

from the fact that I just narrowly avoided a second death, something about that whole ambush still bothers me. That first guy I wasted. His face. I'd recognized him, but thinking on it, I realize he hadn't been in the mugshots on Faye's wall. He'd been in the *picture* on her desk.

I carefully lower my stinging hand to the door handle of the car and lay it there. I place the other deep into the jacket I am wearing.

"You won't be fast enough," Faye says simply. She never looks at me. "My crew is wired into my car just as well as they are into me."

My finger lifts from the trigger of the gun in my jacket, but only slightly, just in case she's bluffing.

"They might, I don't know, electrocute you in your seat," she continues. "Or eject you into the ceiling, breaking your neck. Or maybe even unlock your car door and spill you out onto the pavement at 80 miles per hour. They would make sure to catch your body under the wheels too, of course. They are quite thorough."

She's not bluffing. I take my finger off the trigger and fold my arms across my chest.

"That's better, Mrs. Ramoni. Much more civil. Now. What troubles you?"

"Just another beautiful day in the fucking neighborhood, huh?"

Faye frowns. "If you could be a bit more direct—"

"What 'troubles' me is that I've been taken on a goose chase with no explanation as to what the *fuck* is going on, only to meet a death squad in a fucking candy store!" I snarl. "And that one of the goons in that squad was just smiling at me from your goddamned desk!"

"If you're wondering whether I set you up to be killed, then the answer is no."

"You sure?"

"Obviously, no. Why would we go through all this trouble and use limited resources to bring you back to life *just* to kill you again?"

"Maybe it was just a part of Phase 3 gone wrong."

"No. Not that either. Phase 3 is mental. It's supposed to help you acclimate to your crew."

"Really," I cut my eyes at her, not in the mood for bullshit. "A laffy taffy run is supposed to help my schizophrenia?"

"If you want you and your crew to co-acclimate, you both need to start with small simple tasks. Simple, yet complex tasks."

"How the hell is shopping for candy 'complex'?"

"You do not truly understand the tyranny of choice until the choices themselves, and the people who are to make those choices, become endlessly numerous. Trust me. If you and your crew can agree on what to get out of The Confectionary even once, you'll be well on your way to a happy co-existence. *That* was the point of this whole thing, not... what happened."

Faye's brows knit down, and somehow I know that she's telling the truth. Her explanation of Phase 3 doesn't quite answer all my questions, though, so I continue.

"Faye. If that ambush wasn't apart of Phase 3, then who were those guys, and why were they trying to kill me? Were they those doll monster things I saw in the tank?"

Faye looks at me eyes wide, and I know I've just delivered another piece of bad news. News that she didn't already know. "Please elaborate."

"After you," I snap vengefully.

Her mouth tightens. "The tank you swam in is called an ACC-TANK, "acc" being short for acclimation. It contains chemical compounds, synthetic proteins, and other organic microscopic matter that help to freeze shock your nanites. Not only does that circumvent nanite infection, but it also reprograms them and opens them up to acclimation inside their new host. Nanites suspended in the compound will stay frozen, making them and their host unable to move independently."

"So then those doll things that tried to kill me at the bottom of the tank are—"

"Prisoners."

I turn to her, my gaze solid. My crew was right. Faye *was* lying. "Prisoners. Really."

"Yes. Former Camille agents gone rogue, defective autotech... and others."

"I see," I mutter. It's too early to let on that my crew's got her number. So I'm careful with my next words. "And they can't get out."

"Not while they're inside the tank. So to answer your question, no. Your attackers weren't those 'killer dolls' you speak of. Like I said, the liquid compound makes nanites, and their hosts, dormant. They can't get out."

I don't buy it, and a part of me wonders if Faye even believes her own words. Either she is lying about the dolls being unable to move, or she didn't know what happened when I was in the tank. I decide to test her.

"Newsflash," I snap. "The fact that they 'can't move in the tank'? That's crap. One of them grabbed me and tried to drown me while I was in there."

For the first time, Faye tore her gaze from the road. She looks shocked.

"Yeah." I keep going. "And she looked *pissed*."

"Did you not alert Roi to this?"

"I was barely conscious. Roi dragged me and locked me

in the trunk of her car, so let's say I wasn't feeling gregarious when I next saw her."

"This is troubling. I will have the girls cycle in new fluid when we— no, I'll do it right now." She takes one hand from the wheel and dances her fingers nimbly across the dashboard display. Guess it doesn't take long for the request to file, because a voice comes through the line a second later.

"Got it, Faye." It's Tren. "Are you three on your way back?"

"Nearly there. Listen, I need a population count on the ACC-TANKS."

"Just finished one up, actually!" Tren replies cheerfully. "They're all there, Capn. Sleepin' like babies."

"How long ago was that? When did you last count them?"

"Stayed on schedule, so... that would have been fifteen minutes ago?"

Faye breathes out slowly. If Tren's telling the truth, that meant that not a single "prisoner" had moved from population. Which meant that Faye was right: the guys who'd attacked me weren't those killer doll things. She looks relieved, but this knowledge only gives me partial peace. Drowned killer dolls may not be on my ass, but *someone* is.

"Capn?" Tren's concerned voice spurts through the comm. "You good over there?"

"I'm fine, Tren. Thank you. But if population is still on ice, that means we might have ReO activity in the 17th sector. We need to call a meeting. Stat. We're only ten minutes out, and I want reports on my desk the moment we pull in."

"ReOs... Jesus Christ. Roger that, Captain. We'll be ready for you."

The radio call ends, and I can hear the engine of the car

pick up more speed as Faye leans her foot on the pedal. Now she's glancing into her rearview. Whatever is going on sounds urgent. *Way* more urgent than she is letting on.

I glare at her, waiting for an explanation. When she doesn't give one, I press: "So then these Rios, or whatever. *They* are the things that attacked me?"

"Re. O. Short for the ReOrient. And I'm not quite sure it's time for you to learn that yet. I'm not sure you're ready."

"They came in trying to blow my head off, and my arm turned itself into a particle cannon. A PARTICLE CANNON, Faye. Out of nowhere!"

"Yes, when you told me that, I was equally surprised."

"And they know that Andrea Daanik Ramoni, who is *me*— an accused husband-murdering, plague-making, merchant-of-death, just in case you forgot— is still alive. What little anonymity I had in death has literally just been shot, so honestly I think it's time to tell me what's going on before me being here with you comes down on *all* of us. Who are the ReOrient, and why do they want me dead?"

Faye is silent for a long time. Weighing pros and cons, perhaps. Finally, she relents. "People like us—" she says. "Me, Roi, and now you— we don't just exist on the bleeding edge. We *are* the bleeding edge. The perfect hybrid of man and machine, existing only to keep the balance between the two."

"Yeah, we covered that..." I mutter impatiently.

"Due to advancements we've made on your autotech and nanotech innovations, we can control both our organic and inorganic matter down to the last cell, changing anything about ourselves that we wish. Facial features, body composition."

"Covered that too, saw the demo, let's keep it moving." Yes, I'm a bitch, but I can't help it. Sorry.

Faye ignores me, determined to finish. "And for the more sophisticated Camille, the ones who have the most symbiotic relationships with their crews, we can even change our neural firing patterns and pathways, *change* the very way our brains are wired."

My eyes widen. *This* was new. "Hold the phone. You can literally change the composition of your brain? Like, you wake up one day and decide you want to be more artistic. So you increase the pathways in the right lobe, or whatever, and suddenly you're on some Beethoven-DaVinci shit?"

Faye nods. "That's less sophisticated an explanation than is required to understand such an intricate process—and you being a scientist, I'm surprised you can be so anti-intellectual about it— but in short, yes."

"Wow. Awesome."

Faye nods, but she doesn't look as hyped as I feel about the whole thing. "Yes. It is. We can effectively change our own knowledge, skill sets, muscle memory, and experiential recall. If you try hard enough, you can even completely change your self-identity to the extent that even *you* will truly believe you are another person. The process is called re-simulation, and in ReSim, we can be anything we want to be, Mrs. Ramoni. We maintain control. *That* is why we call ourselves The Camille. Not just because we can change... but because we are in total control of that change."

I stare at her, awed. I can't even imagine what choices I would make, what forms I could take, the new lives I could build, all the things I could accomplish with just a single, focused thought. But Faye's serious expression drowns my world of possibilities.

"I hear a 'but' coming on," I say. "The Re-Os 'use their powers for evil', or some shit like that. Right?"

"Yes, some shit like that." Faye sighs. "Sometimes, in the pursuit of evolution, a Camille can evolve too much and too quickly. There is a state of ReSim that will allow a Camille to evolve in her totality. In this state, a Camille changes *everything* about herself, including who she thinks she is as a person. She forgets herself. She loses her way.

For some, this a philosophical problem. For others, this is a literal biological problem. To change yourself, your knowledge, your personality, your memories... to take these changes too far means to become a completely different person entirely. Sometimes, this new person can take over, effectively killing the original persona. When that happens, you are no longer in ReSim. You are in re-orientation. You are Re-O."

"So The Camille can change herself so much that she literally forgets who she is."

"Exactly. In many instances, she can even become a much darker version of herself, and she wouldn't even remember how she got there. Re-Os are dangerous. Volatile. They risk exposing us to the outside world, but more importantly, they risk destroying The Camille altogether."

My lips part, loathe to ask the question. But finally they do. "Starting with me?"

"The ReOrient have been a problem for The Camille ever since our inception. Your presence did not instigate that."

"Well, I must have pissed *someone* off, because apparently, they knew we were coming. They knew I was coming, and they wanted to make sure I wasn't walking out of there alive."

"Shouldn't be a problem for you, though. Rehab and release, right?" Faye says softly. "That's what you wanted? To be healed and let go?"

I bite down, as much from frustration as from my refusal to eat my own words. She's right: flying off into freedom isn't looking so hot right now. Even if I *could* still use my new "features" to protect myself, spending my life looking over my shoulder was not how I wanted to roll. I might as well be that dirty kid living in the library bathroom again.

I sigh and squeeze my eyes shut, relenting. "Fine. I'll stay. I will train, and I will become a Camille. But only as long as it's mutually beneficial." Then I look at her, hard. "The moment I feel like shit's going off its rocker around here, and that I'm better off on my own? I'm out. With no fuss. Deal?"

Faye seems to consider my bargain. Then she nods. "Deal. Though, considering the circumstances, if 'shit goes off rockers' as you say, then we're *all* 'out'. And with very much fuss, as it happens."

I have no idea what she's talking about, but it doesn't sound good. To be fair, she's been trying to tell me what's been happening in her world, and I, like an asshole, haven't been listening. Maybe it was time to start.

"Well," I mutter. "At least we're in the same boat now." My words aren't the best olive branch, but when she smiles, I realize she's taken it. Good enough. "So what's next?"

"We swear you in officially as a Camille. Then, I'll tell you everything. Then, you train."

"Fair enough." And as ridiculous as my next demand is, I mean every single word. "I'll need my car," I say. "A big ass drink too, if you don't mind. And it'd better not be a milkshake."

Faye smirks. "Deal. Welcome to the family."

"Sure, whatever." I look out the window. "Cap'n."

We say no more to each other, and while I can't see it, I

can feel the warmth of her smile filling the car. I brace my foot on the dash, lean my head on my window, and gaze at the sinking sun. This new world is strange, psychotic. But it is also free. I am free. Though I carry myself wherever I go, I can be whoever I want now. In a weird way, I am once again that street kid in the library bathroom. Lost. Rootless. But this time, I have people watching my back... and I have cannons.

I think of my new "family". I think of Faye, who's been spending all her time trying to answer these questions for me and trying to get me to see that something bigger than all of us is coming. Of Chica, who somehow knows much but keeps all secrets. Of Roi, who hates me, and of Tren who seems to think I'm some weird new pet. I think of my tantrums, and of how I haven't been making anyone's job here any easier.

I think of how I'm going to change all that.

Well... I'm going to try, at least. So long as me and "Mildred" can continue to agree on mutual survival, I think we can manage.

I look at my hand again, knowing its power, wondering about its potential. My potential. The nanites and I are now one, a seamless melding of man and machine. I feel good. Whole. My body feels as strong as it used to be. *Stronger*, even. I have no idea what's coming, but for now, all I know is gratitude. Because for the second time, I live. *We* live.

I close my eyes against the road, and I smile. Tears slide down my cheeks. "We live."

ABOUT COLBY

A shameless nerd and bookworm since the age of five, Colby R. Rice is a sci-fi and fantasy author, screenwriter, director, afro-puffed kitchen ninja, and founder of Rebel Ragdoll, a media f'empire in progress!

———

If you enjoyed 'The Camille'
you'll love Colby's dystopian thriller series
'The Books of Ezekiel'.

Grab the first novel FREE!

———

Get notified of giveaways & new releases by signing up to Colby's mailing list at:

http://www.colbyrrice.com/

facebook.com/ColbyRRicePage

twitter.com/ColbyRRice

instagram.com/colbyrrice

amazon.com/author/colbyrice

youtube.com/colbyrrice

goodreads.com/colbyrrice

pinterest.com/colbyrrice